REDEMPTION OF A MARQUESS

THE MARRIAGE MAKER BOOK SEVEN THE RULES OF REFINEMENT

TARAH SCOTT

ISBN-13: 978-1-953100-30-6

www.scarsdalepublishing.com

Cover design by dreams2media & R. Jackson Designs

Editor Casey Yager

First Trade Paperback Printing by Scarsdale Publishing 2018

10 9 8 7 6 5 4 3 2

SP

RULES OF REFINEMENT

Noblemen aren't always honorable... but a rake is always charming

In a narrow lane off Edinburgh's illustrious Charlotte Square, stands a town house that is not quite as impressive as nearby residences, but remains a place of distinction. An air of quiet dignity is maintained by the courtyard that fronts the street, while privacy is assured by a wrought-iron gateway. This house is Lady Peddington's School for Young Ladies and is owned and run by Lady Honoria Peddington.

Girls fortunate enough to attend the academy are instructed in all aspects of proper comportment with emphasis on the importance of a pleasing demeanor and appearance, grace and good manners, the skills a lady needs to run a large, well-to-do household, and – of course - the necessity and advantages of an impeccable reputation. Scandal, the girls are warned, must be avoided at all costs.

Lady Peddington's own reputation is the finest, and all Edinburgh considers her above reproach. She is especially well-loved by the affluent merchants and lesser gentry who live on the fringes of the city's New Town where she operates her school. These clients appreciate her knack at finding affluent husbands for their daughters. No one suspects that her knowledge of men comes from the long-ago days when she wasn't Lady Honoria Peddington, but simply Honey Pedding who ran a well-doing Glasgow brothel.

Those skills, though secret, still serve her well, for when her school's famed graduation balls fail to secure suitable husbands for some of her more high-spirited girls, other gentlemen come to the fore, eager to accept these gems as pampered mistresses. So, however a girl's heart might lean, Lady Peddington's School for Young Ladies guarantees happiness for all.

CHAPTER 1

VALAN GREY, THE 6ᵀᴴ EARL OF EDMONDS, THE MARQUESS OF Northington, sipped wine and watched the brown-haired beauty waltz with Mr. Evans, a peacock amid a glittering barnyard of hens. Evans had twice stepped on her toes, yet her smile hadn't faltered. Valan slowed his stroll and spared a glance for the other wolf, almost a pup, that prowled near the open balcony doors. A breeze ruffled the young man's styled blond locks. The youth of today relied far too much on well-made coats and coiffured hair in an effort to catch a lady's attention. Any man of worth understood that what lay beneath the coat mattered far more to a lady of taste. He returned his attention to the beauty. Her partner turned to the music. Valan winced. Evans' step was off by half a beat.

Between pale satin dresses, the swirl of the beauty's emerald velvet skirt molded around her firm buttocks before she was lost from view in the sea of dancers. Had Lady Peddington suggested the dress? The beauty certainly stood out amongst the demure pastels that flared on the dance floor. She was older than the others who attended the Midnight Ball. *Perfect.* Tomorrow, he would send a letter of thanks to Honoria for her invitation to the soiree. She had a knack for knowing just the right lady for a gentleman.

Above the music and murmur of guests, a female gasp was followed by a man's curse. Valan glanced left, toward the small commotion, but a half-closed curtain hid the man and woman in the alcove. He shifted his gaze back to the dance floor. A blur in the corner of his eye registered an instant too late, and a woman collided with him. Wine sloshed over the rim of his glass and onto his crisply pressed, ivory silk waistcoat. He seized the lady's wrist to stop her fall.

Valan glanced down at the now ruined waistcoat, then met the young woman's wide-eyed gaze. "I assume you learned enough etiquette at Lady Peddington's to know that it's bad manners to collide with guests. Or is this your way of gaining an introduction?"

Her brown eyes flicked to the wine-stained waistcoat then back to his face. The fear in her gaze flashed into annoyance. "I do not want an introduction."

"Where is that bitch?" A large man lunged past the alcove curtain, half limping.

Valan deftly sidestepped him, pulling the young woman with him. Viscount Hesston stumbled two paces, narrowly missing two ladies. They cast him frowns and hurried past as he whirled.

He came up short when his gaze met Valan's. "What the devil are you doing here, Northington? Didn't think this sort of place was one of your usual haunts." The music ended and the last words were overloud in the absence of the orchestra. The viscount's eyes narrowed on the young woman. "Looking for another victim, little pigeon?" He grabbed for her.

Valan tugged her out of her assailant's reach. "This 'little pigeon' is otherwise engaged."

The man's face contorted in rage. "She is mine. I've spent the evening with her. She *owes* me."

Valan glanced where he'd last seen the beauty on the dance floor. Gone. No doubt, claimed by the young wolf. With a sigh, he returned his attention to Hesston. "Ownership is a matter of perspective. As she has ruined a very expensive waistcoat, I believe she *owes* me."

She tugged in an effort to break free. Valan held tight and nodded at a passing waiter.

"My claim supersedes yours," Hesston said as the waiter stopped beside them.

Valan set his wine glass on the waiter's tray.

"I d-do no' belong to either of y-you," the girl said.

The waiter frowned. Valan ignored him and turned curious eyes on her. "Where are you from, child?"

"That is none of your c-concern," she said.

"Perhaps not," he replied, "but indulge me."

She shook her head.

"Would you rather go with this man?" He nodded at Hesston, whose face reddened.

"She is mine," the viscount growled.

"Patience," Valan said. "She may choose to go with you, in which case I will not interfere."

"You have no right to interfere, at all," Hesston snapped.

Valan turned cold eyes on him. "Even you can wait sixty seconds." He looked at the girl and lifted a brow in question.

She glanced at Hesston, then looked back at him and shook her head. "N-nae."

"There you have it," he said. "Even at Lady Peddington's Midnight Ball, a lady is free to choose her companions."

Hesston cast a disgruntled look at her. "Dumb bitch," he muttered.

She lifted her chin. "I would rather be dumb than cruel."

The remark earned her a disdainful look from a woman strolling by on the arm of a man.

Hesston again lunged for her. Valan stepped between them.

"You're drunk, Hesston. Go home before you irritate the wrong person."

"Like you?" he sneered.

Valan shrugged. "I am not the best shot in Edinburgh."

"Damn right, you're not," he growled.

"I am more likely to set a runner on you," he said.

Hesston's eyes widened. "They hunt criminals. I have never committed a crime in my life."

"That is a matter of perspective."

A vicious glint lit Hesston's eyes. "If that is so, then one might contend that you stepped outside the law on at least *one* occasion. Last I heard, marriage to an underage woman is against the law," Hesston said.

Ah, the viscount had heard that Valan's old nemesis had returned to Edinburgh just today. Gossip traveled fast when *Society* smelled blood.

Valan gave a bland smile. "Then I am fortunate not to have committed that crime."

"You tried hard enough," Hesston declared.

"Even I do not always succeed," Valan remarked.

"You succeeded at winning your fortune in a card game," he snarled. "That is highly illegal."

"A friendly game of cards is never illegal," Valan said, then added before he could reply, "The important point to remember, my dear viscount, is that runners give an ear to high-ranking peers."

The man's face twisted into a scowl. "You think well of yourself."

Valan angled his head." I am on excellent terms with Bow Street."

Hesston took a step back. "You pay them well, is what you mean." He sneered at the girl. "A bit of muslin isn't worth this much trouble."

"I am no bit of muslin," she retorted.

Hesston turned, stumbled past a group of men, then hurried away.

Valan looked down at the young lady. "You cost me a great deal tonight."

Her brow furrowed. "The cost of that waistcoat is a pittance for a man like you."

He thought of the brown-haired beauty. "Money is not the only thing of worth in this world, child."

"I am no' a child."

He arched a brow. "Pray tell, how old are you?"

"Nineteen."

"A nineteen-year-old girl who nearly got herself accosted by a rather nasty viscount."

"Release me." She yanked the wrist he still gripped.

He started when something pricked his wrist. Valan drew her hand upward. She yanked harder and nearby guests glanced their way. Valan offered them a chilly smile, then urged the girl back three paces nearer the alcove.

"I beg your pardon," she began, then broke off when he tightened his grip.

He turned her hand over and forced her fingers apart. A modest diamond stick pin balanced halfway across her palm.

Valan looked at her and raised a questioning brow. "That is a gentleman's pin, if I am not mistaken."

Her mouth thinned in a mutinous line.

"Shall I call Viscount Hesston back and ask if he has lost a diamond pin?" he asked.

Her eyes widened. "Nae. D-do not do that. Please."

Valan lifted the pin from her palm then released her. "I assume, then, the good viscount did not give this to you as a token of his, er, undying love?"

"Undying love?" she scoffed. "That man loves only himself."

He repressed a smile. "Forgive me, but I am curious as to how you came to be in possession of his pin. It's unlikely he removed it in order to disrobe. Removal of his cravat would not be necessary to—"

"He did not give it to me," she cut in.

"Then you slipped it from his cravat when he kissed you?"

She lifted her chin. "Ladies do not allow strange men to kiss them."

"How wonderful to know you recognize some conduct befitting a lady. I suggest you remember that when next a man asks you to accompany him to an alcove."

She dropped her gaze. Ah, he had her. She slanted a look up at him through her lashes and it was easy to see why she had captured Hesston's attention. Her innocence was a lure few men could resist. She extended a hand toward him and stepped forward. Then tripped. She cried out and collided with him. His lapel tugged downward when she grabbed him and Valan caught her.

He set her at arm's length. "That is the second time this evening you have landed in my arms." He tugged his cravat back into place, then felt the knot in an effort to assess the damage. "Perhaps we should be formally introduced before a third *encounter*?" Valan paused, then felt along the length of the cravat. His pin— He lowered his hands to his sides and leveled an assessing gaze on her. "My pin, please."

Her eyes sparkled as she opened her left hand. His ruby pin lay on her palm.

Valan took the pin. "It is not often I am shocked, but you have managed to shock me."

The laughter in her eyes vanished and her back went ramrod straight. "A gentleman would give me a head start."

He paused while slipping both pins into the front pocket of his coat. "A head start?"

"Before ye call Bow Street."

A corner of his mouth twitched again, harder. He removed

his hand from his pocket. "You are safe, my child. I do not set Bow Street on the scent of young ladies."

She studied him as if uncertain, then her expression cleared, and she flashed a brilliant smile. "You are kind—despite the austere face." Before he could reply, she added, "Admit it, once you discovered the pin missing, you would have assumed you lost it by accident and would no' have suspected me—just as that evil viscount will not."

"Fortune favors you on that score," Valan said. "Hesston would not hesitate to have you arrested—if, that is, you failed to comply with his demands."

She frowned. "Demands? Oh, you mean, he would make me his mistress."

"Nothing so elevated as that, but never mind. Dare I ask how you came to have this, er, talent?"

She shrugged, but a steel determination underlay the nonchalance. "A woman develops skills necessary to survive."

"Aye," he agreed. "Women are very adept at surviving. I take it, then, you need the money."

She frowned. "I do not steal for money. Well, not for myself. By-the-by, please return my pin."

He lifted a brow. "*Your* pin?"

"It certainly isn't yours," she said.

"Neither is it yours," he said.

"Finders keepers."

"Is that what you call your talent, 'finding'?"

She scowled. "You don't need it."

"My dear, if you pawn this pin, you will surely find yourself hunted by Bow Street. Unless—tell me, have you already a relationship with a pawn broker?"

She gave him a haughty stare. "I do not."

"Then we shall not begin now."

She shook her head. "Everyone thinks they know what is best for me. I don't not want—"

Valan grimaced. "Pray, say no more. Surely, Miss Peddington taught you not to use double negatives in a sentence."

She dropped her gaze. "Aye, she did."

"Will you throw away every penny your father spent to send you here by speaking like a common fishwife?"

"M-my mother sent me here."

Valan regarded her. "Do you only stutter when you're afraid?"

Her cheeks reddened even as her chin lifted. "I cannot help it. If you don't like it—" her cheeks pinked more "—then you are no gentleman."

"Your judgment of what constitutes a gentleman is sorely misguided." She opened her mouth to reply, but he lifted a hand, palm out. "Please, we will save that discussion for another time. I happen to agree. You cannot help the stutter. You can, however, choose the words you speak. I suggest you make a habit of choosing them more carefully."

Movement beyond the girl's shoulder drew Valan's attention. He recognized the tall man who approached. "Wedded bliss losing its luster so soon?" Valan asked when Sir Stirling James reached them.

Stirling grinned. "Not at all." He looked pointedly at the young lady.

"I cannot make introductions," Valan said. "I don't know the young lady's name."

"Then allow me." Stirling bowed. "Miss Jeanine Matheson, I am Sir Stirling James, and this is his Lordship, the Marquess of Northington."

She extended her hand and Valan bowed over it. "A marquess?" she said. "You did not tell me you were a peer."

"You did not ask," he said, then looked at Stirling. "Do you know all the young ladies? Never say you come here often."

Stirling shook his head. "I saw ye two together. Honoria told me who she was."

"Ah," Valan intoned. "It is Lady Peddington you came to visit."

"Honoria and I are old friends," Stirling said. "Not *that* kind of old friends," he added when Valan started to reply. "But if we were, the past is the past."

Valan angled his head. "As you say."

"You knew Lady Peddington before she started the school?" Miss Matheson asked.

Stirling smiled. "Indeed, I did."

"I want to have a school like this someday," she said.

"Good God, why?" Valan asked.

"To be an independent woman. Lady Peddington says a lady will do best if she finds a nice gentleman to care for her. But that is not what she did. She started the school. She makes her own money and spends it any way she pleases."

"Much responsibility comes with running a business," Valan said.

She waved her hand dismissively. "Running a gentleman's household is just as big a responsibility."

"When a lady has a gentleman to look after her, she has someone to care for her should something go wrong," he said.

She frowned. "I have known too many ladies whose husbands do not take care of them."

"She has you there, Northington," Stirling said.

"That she does," Valan said. "On that note, I shall say goodnight."

"Leaving so early?" Stirling asked.

"Aye. The hunt is finished for tonight." He looked at the young lady. "Good evening, Miss Matheson."

She took a step toward him. "Must you go?"

He flashed a bland smile. "Old gentlemen need their rest."

She grimaced. "You are not old."

"Old enough."

"The choice of gentlemen to dance with has dwindled," she said. "I hoped perhaps…"

"Perhaps his lordship will dance with you." He nodded at Stirling.

She frowned at Stirling. "Lordship? You introduced yourself as Sir Stirling James."

"He is both," Valan said. "The marquess suffers an unnatural modesty. He seldom admits his title."

"The title is a courtesy, and hardly signifies," Stirling said.

Valan glimpsed Hesston talking with Lady Peddington near the far right wall, not far from a cluster of ladies. Valan returned his attention to Miss Matheson. "The marquess is probably the only gentleman present. If, that is, he's still a gentleman."

Stirling chuckled. "You would have to ask Chastity."

"Chastity?" she asked.

"His wife," Valan said.

"You're married?" The young lady wrinkled her nose. "Then it will not do for me to dance with you."

"You are refreshingly forthright," Stirling said.

"She is naïve," Valan said. "A married man has his uses."

She narrowed her eyes. "Are you married?"

"Nae, and I have no wish to be. Goodnight, Miss Matheson. Sir Stirling." He bowed and left.

CHAPTER 2

AS SOON AS VALAN ARRIVED AT LADY DOUGLAS'S BALL, HE BEGAN to think that his steward had erred in suggesting he attend—until he spotted the same dark-haired beauty he'd seen at Lady Peddington's ball two nights ago. He retired to the shadows of one of the ballroom's ridiculous columns and watched the beauty dance a reel with Viscount Chilson. When she began a second dance with the viscount, Valan knew he had made a dishonest woman of her. Chilson was short and stout. A dishonest woman would no doubt prefer a tall, handsome lover—if only for an evening.

The music rose above the murmur of voices as the dancers' steps picked up speed.

Chilson wouldn't last more than two sets. Already, his face was flushed. As was his habit, he would play cards and lose five hundred pounds before the night ended.

"Northington, I thought that was you." The Earl of Davon stopped in front of him. "I thought, perhaps, you were hiding here," he said.

Valan kept his eyes on the dark-haired beauty. "Yet you came to speak with me."

"Well, yes—surely you aren't truly hiding?" the earl said. "I was only joking."

Valan sighed. "Of course, you were."

"Here, now," Davon said. "There's no need to be rude."

The dark-haired beauty disappeared behind a cluster of dancers. The dance would last another three minutes.

Valan looked at the earl. "You are right, of course. Was there something you wanted?"

The man blinked. "Well, no. I was just being friendly."

"Thank you," Valan said. "If you will excuse me, there is a lady in need of my services."

"Your services?" he began, but Valan left him standing beside the column and headed for the opposite side of the room.

He reached the spot where Viscount Chilson had exited the dance floor with the lady on his arm.

"Of course, my dear," Chilson was saying. "You may have all the champagne you like." He tweaked her nose. They reached the refreshments table. The viscount picked up a glass of champagne and handed it to her. "You may rest with the other ladies," he said, and added in a whisper, "Remember, you're my cousin's daughter visiting from Bath."

So that was the excuse he used to explain his mistress's presence at a society ball. He had no wife to complain of his indiscretions. Still, the story wouldn't gain them entrance to more than two or three parties, for no reputable hostess wanted her party sullied by the presence of a man's mistress.

Valan chose a glass of champagne and faced the dancers. From the corner of his eye, he observed Chilson guide his young mistress to a chair near a corner occupied by other ladies. He tweaked her nose again and Valan couldn't help but envision the earl tweaking her nose while he puffed, out of breath, on top of her. Valan half wandered if the earl had yet deflowered her.

Chilson left and no one spoke to the girl. No doubt, many knew *what* she was. Valan finished his champagne, then placed the glass on a nearby table and strode toward her chair. Her head snapped up and she looked at him, her brow furrowed in confusion.

"Would you care to dance?" he asked.

She glanced uncertainly in the direction Chilson had disappeared. "I do not know."

Her voice, low and sultry, matched her dark beauty. He might have to steal her from Chilson. "Have you promised this dance to another?" he asked.

She shook her head.

"You do dance?" he asked.

She nodded.

He lifted a brow. "Do you speak?"

Her cheeks colored. She started to nod, then stopped, and said, "I speak."

"And you dance?" he said.

"And I dance," she replied.

He extended a hand toward her. "The set will soon begin."

She placed her fingers in his, then rose. He led her to the dance floor and they joined a group on the edge. She stood across from him, eyes on his chest instead of his face. Either Chilson hadn't deflowered her or he had been unkind when he did.

The music began and, as he'd already observed, she danced well. That pleased him. A smile twitched the corner of his mouth. Perhaps he would bring her to balls like this one. He would, no doubt, attend at least half a dozen soirées before doors closed to him. Perhaps they wouldn't close at all. Being wealthy had its advantages.

When the dance ended, Valan slipped her hand into the crook of his arm and led her through the open balcony doors. A dozen other guests milled about the balcony. She cast a nervous glance toward the ballroom and slowed. Valan placed his hand over hers, keeping her fingers firmly wrapped around his arm. She was forced to walk alongside him as they descended the steps to the lawn.

"I do not think that I should come out here with you, my lord," she said.

"Why not?"

"Viscount Chilson won't like it."

"Then we shan't tell him. Do you like gardens?"

"Gardens are beautiful, of course. But a lady—"

"Viscount Chilson's cousin's daughter?" he cut in.

She looked sharply at him.

He flashed the smile that had earned him the name *The Morning Star.* "Would you prefer Viscount Chilson's company to mine?"

She regarded him for a long moment as he slowed their steps across the lawn. "May I ask who you are, sir?"

"Valan Grey, the 6th Earl of Edmonds, the Marquess of Northington."

"An earl *and* a marquess?" she said in a breathless voice.

He nodded, slightly disconcerted that it was his title that captured her attention and not his smile. He was getting old.

"You are more handsome that Viscount Chilson," she murmured.

"You are too kind," he said with a sardonic smile.

They left the lights of the mansion and entered a pebbled path lined by flowers. Moonlight illuminated her face. They had gone far enough. Valan slipped an arm around her waist and began lowering his head to hers.

"You are no gentleman!" a woman shrilled.

Valan stilled. Surely that wasn't…

The bushes up ahead rustled violently, and a small form broke through at a rapid walk, headed toward them. The dark-haired beauty stiffened as the woman approached.

"Lydia?" The newcomer reached them and stopped. "Is that you?"

A large figure emerged from the bushes, but turned in the opposite direction and disappeared around a hedge.

"What are you doing here in the garden?" Miss Matheson asked.

"The same thing you are, it seems," Lydia replied.

Miss Matheson looked at him and frowned. "*Y-you.*"

"I see you did not heed my warning about going off alone with a man, Miss Matheson."

"You know her?" The dark-haired beauty stepped from his embrace. She glanced from Miss Matheson to him.

"Miss Matheson and I met the other night at Lady Peddington's Midnight Ball."

"Met the other night—" Lydia turned to face Miss Matheson. "What are you doing here?"

"I was trying to take a walk—"

"Not that," she cut in. "What are you doing at this party?"

"I was invited, just like you."

"Not like me, I think," Lydia snapped, and looked at Valan. "You invited her?"

"This is not my party."

Lydia slipped her hand into the crook of his arm and addressed Miss Matheson. "Lord Northington and I are going for a stroll. Find your own gentleman."

Miss Matheson laughed. "What a wicked girl you are, Lydia. I saw you in the ballroom with that short, pudgy gentleman. You were not at all proper. Now you are walking in the gardens with a different gentleman."

"How interesting that you notice impropriety in others," Valan said.

"I did not come to the garden with a gentleman," Miss Matheson said. "So, I am not guilty of impropriety."

"How dare you?" Lydia breathed. She tugged his arm. "Are you going to let her speak to me in that manner?"

"You are angry only because it's true," Miss Matheson said.

Lydia stamped her foot. "I can't help it if gentlemen like me better than you."

"It isn't *you* they like, Lydia."

Valan forced back laughter, unable to speak for fear of encouraging the lass. His efforts were in vain, however, for she cocked her head and said, "See, even his lordship agrees with me."

The dark-haired beauty drew in a sharp breath. "A true gentleman would not allow a lady to be spoken to in this manner."

"If I were a gentleman, I wouldn't be here with you in the garden," he replied. "As for you being a lady…"

She yanked her hand free and took a step back. "I have never been treated so shabbily." Without another word, she whirled and marched back toward the mansion.

Valan watched her retreat for two heartbeats, then faced Miss Matheson. "You have a knack for interfering with my plans. Tell me, who invited you to Lady Douglas's ball?"

"Lady Douglas, of course."

"The two of you are acquainted?" he asked in surprise. Perhaps, like Lydia, she had found herself a protector.

"Lady Peddington sometimes obtains invitations for us to attend other balls," she said.

"Does Lady Douglas not chaperone you?" he asked.

"She filled my dance card and sent me off. I have been dancing for two hours. My feet hurt, and I am tired. I came out here for some fresh air. That *gentleman* found me and was not very polite."

"Neither were you, my dear," Valan said.

"What? Should I have let him take liberties?"

"It didn't occur to you that you should not be out here at all, that perhaps it wasn't proper?" he asked.

"A lady shouldn't have to fear being accosted when she takes a walk."

He tsked. "I fear you've wasted the money your poor mother spent to send you to Lady Peddington's school. How do you propose to teach young women to become ladies when you do not act the part?"

"Oh, that. I need no' be a lady to own a school."

"Interesting logic. Where, pray tell, will you get the money for this school?"

She glanced around as if to be certain no one listened, then leaned close and said, "I plan to marry a very old, rich gentleman."

He stared. "Marriage to a rich gentleman. A time-honored tradition among ladies. Come." He grasped her arm and began walking toward the mansion. "For your plan to succeed, you must not be caught in these gardens with the likes of me."

"That is silly," she said. "You have been nothing but a gentleman. No one could accuse you of being improper."

She practically trotted to keep up with him, but he didn't slow. "If we do not reach the ballroom unseen, you may discover how wrong you are."

"This is the first time a gentleman has tried to drag me *back* into a ballroom," she said.

"It is a first for me, as well," he said dryly.

"Then why do it?"

He gave her a thin-lipped look. "You would prefer I drag you into the bushes?"

"Nae," she replied. "I was just curious."

"Surely, you know that curiosity killed the cat," he said. "Did your mother teach you not to trust strange men?"

"Oh, I learned that on my own—and you usually can't trust those you know, either."

"For one so cynical, you are naïve to enter any garden alone."

"I think you are the one who is naïve," she said. "Most men don't need gardens to become forward."

He couldn't help a hearty laugh. "I stand corrected."

They turned a corner in the path and came face-to-face with another couple. Valan cursed before the moonlight revealed the couple as Sir Stirling and his wife.

"Your lordship." He gave a slight bow. "My lady. I understand congratulations are in order."

Lady Chastity smiled. "Yes, thank you. Ella is a hearty baby."

"I see you are hard at work, as always, Northington," Stirling said with laughter in his voice. "Miss Matheson, fancy seeing you here. You and the marquess seem to be getting along well."

"Miss Matheson was lost," Valan said. "I happened upon her and am escorting her back to the mansion."

"Why don't I see her back?" Lady Chastity said.

"That would be best, ma'am." Valan canted his head in gratitude.

"But—" Miss Matheson began.

"Go along," he cut in. "It is far better you are seen returning to the party with Lady Chastity than with me." She shook her head and he added, "Remember your plans."

She pouted prettily, but nodded. "I will go, this once. But don't think you can order me about."

"Heaven forbid," he said, and the two women left.

"You are fortunate it was Chastity and I who happened upon ye," Stirling said as they trailed the ladies at a leisurely pace.

"Far more fortunate for her than I," Valan said.

"That is most assuredly true," he said, making no effort to hide his amusement. "What is she doing here?"

"It seems Honoria secured her an invitation to the ball."

"Interesting," Stirling said. "I had no idea her services extended to securing ladies invitations to private parties. What were you referring to when you told her, 'remember your plans'?"

"She hopes to finance a school by marrying a wealthy gentleman who will promptly die and leave her his money."

Stirling looked sharply at him. "Are you serious?"

"She confessed the plan herself."

"Well, the girl is industrious."

"She is silly," Valan said.

"Perhaps, but there are worse plans. Speaking of which, I hear you intend to visit London for an extended stay."

Valan shook his head. "Nae, I try to have as few plans as possible. Where did you hear that?"

"Chastity told me, if I recall."

Valan cast him a sidelong glance. Sir Stirling James wasn't known for engaging in gossip—though plenty of gossip surrounded the man who more and more people referred to as The Marriage Maker.

They reached the balcony steps, ascended, then entered the ballroom. They stopped just inside the double doors and Sir Stirling scanned the crowd.

"Chastity probably took Miss Matheson to the ladies' retiring room," he said. "We will likely not see them again for some time."

"More likely, I will not see Miss Matheson again," Valan said.

"Unless she finds herself a rich old gentleman," Stirling said.

Valan laughed. "I wish her luck." His gaze caught on a tall man talking with two others. Cold uncoiled in his gut. At last, the evening had gotten interesting.

"I met Lord Gordon yesterday at a luncheon," Stirling said. "He's just returned from England after being away for..." Stirling looked at Valan.

"Eighteen years," Valan finished for him.

The curtain on an alcove a few feet to the left of Lord Gordon parted and Lady Chastity and Miss Matheson stepped out. Gordon turned toward them, said something to his companion, then took three steps to the alcove. He bowed over Lady Chastity's hand. She made introductions to Miss Matheson. Gordon lifted Miss Matheson's hand. Valan noticed the extra seconds Gordon held the girl's hand.

"Lord Gordon is no' an elderly gentleman with only a few years left," Stirling said. "Miss Matheson would do better if a man took her on as his ward."

Valan looked at him. "What man would do such a thing?"

Stirling shrugged. "A man who wanted to ensure she didn't fall prey to Lord Gordon."

"You don't like him," Valan said.

"I know little of him. But his attentions strike me as unwholesome." Stirling frowned. "I seem to remember there is bad blood between you two."

"Between Gordon and I?" Valan recalled Gordon's words that fateful night twenty years ago, *"His father shot himself and left him penniless,"* but smiled politely and said, "Nothing more than boyhood mischief. We haven't seen one another since our university days."

Curiosity flickered across Stirling's face, then he flashed white teeth. "Shall we say hello?"

Valan angled his head in acquiescence. "To do otherwise, would be rude."

Stirling lifted his eyebrows in obvious amusement, the gesture, Valan thought, almost as practiced as his own. Valan followed him to the alcove. They approached Gordon's back, which suited Valan well. When they neared, Lady Chastity looked past Gordon's shoulder and Gordon turned. Valan was rewarded with a glimpse of Gordon's shock—and unguarded anger.

Gordon immediately turned his attention to Sir Stirling and bowed. "Your lordship, it is a pleasure to see you again."

"And you, Lord Gordon," Stirling replied. "You know Lord Northington?"

A corner of Gordon's mouth went grim, but he nodded stiffly in Valan's direction.

"Gordon and I are old friends," Valan murmured. "We attended the University of Edinburgh together."

Frustration flashed in Gordon's eyes and Valan repressed a smile. It seemed some things never changed. When Gordon's brother unexpectedly became Viscount Dryer twenty-two years ago, it became a point of pride for Gordon that he be recognized as 'Lord Gordon.'

"I did not know you attended university in Edinburgh, Lord Gordon," Lady Chastity said.

"My father insisted I study business," he replied.

"What did you study, Lord Northington?" she asked

"Nothing so illustrious as business. Art and poetry."

"I do not believe it," Miss Matheson said.

Everyone looked at her.

"May I ask why?" Valan asked.

"You are not at all romantic."

"She is perceptive for one so young," Sir Stirling murmured with a laugh.

Valan regarded her. "As you do not know me, I wonder what brought you to this conclusion."

"As a woman of sense, Miss Matheson can see that you are not a romantic," Gordon said.

"You say that as if being unromantic is a bad thing," Valan maintained a contemplative voice intended to incite him.

Gordon's mouth thinned. "You wouldn't understand the difference."

"His lordship understands the difference perfectly well," Miss Matheson said.

Once again, everyone looked at her.

"Pray tell, how do you know?" Valan asked.

She offered a smug smile. "As a woman of *sense*, I can see that you are intelligent enough to understand what romance is —even if you aren't romantic."

Valan laughed. "Far be it from me to argue with a woman."

"Woman?" Gordon said. "She is barely out of the schoolroom."

Miss Matheson scowled. "I am nineteen, a full-grown woman. I have two younger sisters. One married at eighteen, the other at seventeen. I am an old maid."

"An old maid?" Valan grimaced. "If you are an old maid, then I am ancient."

She rolled her eyes. "Age is different for men."

"How very fortunate for us," Valan said.

"How fortunate, indeed," Lady Chastity said in a dry tone.

The orchestra began a waltz. Miss Matheson looked at the dancers, longing in her eyes, then shifted her gaze to Valan. "We learned the waltz at Lady Peddington's. Will you dance with me?"

"A lady does not ask a gentleman to dance," he admonished. "She waits for a gentleman to ask her."

"But a lady might wait forever," she said.

He tweaked one of her curls. "You will not wait long, trust me, my dear."

"Be warned, Miss Matheson," Gordon said, "a true gentleman does not touch a lady's hair in public." He bowed. "May I have the honor of this dance?"

She looked to Valan and Gordon's cheeks reddened.

"Trust me," Gordon persisted. "We shall dance and have refreshments, then I will see that you arrive home safely."

"How very entertaining," Valan drawled. "I believe Gordon hopes to become your protector, my dear. Never fear—" Valan flashed Gordon a smile "—she has a protector."

CHAPTER 3

SATISFACTION RUSHED THROUGH VALAN WHEN UNDERSTANDING registered in Gordon's eyes.

Lady Chastity looked at her husband and Valan glimpsed the tiny shake of Stirling's head an instant before Gordon addressed Valan, "You think yourself so clever."

"Excuse me," Miss Matheson said, "But—"

Gordon swung his gaze onto Sir Stirling. "She is an innocent, my lord. You cannot allow Northington to make her his mistress."

Valan widened his eyes. "Mistress?" he repeated in unison with Miss Matheson.

Her eyes snapped onto him, but he kept his stare on Gordon. "You misunderstand, Gordon. She is not my mistress. She is my ward."

Gordon gaped. "Your ward?"

"Forgive me." Valan gave a tiny bow. "That is a gross misunderstanding and completely my fault. I should have clarified earlier."

"No misunderstanding, I wager," Gordon muttered. "We all know your reputation as *The Morning Star*."

Valan flashed a broad smile. "The Morning Star was considered the most beautiful of all God's creations."

Anger born of thirty years of envy flashed in Gordon's eyes. "Aye, you are arrogant enough to believe that of yourself."

"You give me too much credit," Valan said. "I have never held myself in such high esteem."

"Oh, but you do—and you do not deny the nickname."

"Excuse me, Lord Gordon, but this is not your business." Miss Matheson gave a dismissive wave of her hand. "Go away."

Valan struggled to maintain a neutral expression.

"You will thank me, Miss Matheson," Gordon replied tightly, then said to Sir Stirling, "My lord, I appeal to your sense of duty. Northington cannot be allowed sway in this young woman's life."

"I find this wildly amusing," Valan interjected. "It seems Gordon would like to reinterpret the law."

A group of ladies passed close by. Once they left earshot, Gordon said, "I happen to know, sir, that Miss Matheson is a student of Lady Peddington's School for Young Ladies and she is no relation to you."

"Indeed?" said Valan. "I am all agog. How is it you find yourself in possession of this knowledge and what has it to do with anything?"

"That is none of your concern. All that matters is that your so-called guardianship is a ruse to take advantage of her."

"You are very rude," said Miss Matheson with heat. "His lordship has been a perfect gentleman. Why, when he found me in the garden, he was very adamant that I return to the ballroom before my reputation was ruined."

"Found you in the gardens?" A glint appeared in Gordon's eyes and his gaze shifted to Valan. "I will not allow you to take advantage of *another* unsuspecting woman."

"One might wonder, my dear Gordon, how you propose to

stop me were that my plan." Valan lifted a brow. "With a pistol, perhaps?"

"That method worked in the past."

"The inexperience of youth, do you not agree?" Valan laughed. "In truth, you saved me much grief by intervening that night."

Gordon blinked. "I beg your pardon?"

"Victoria and I didn't suit at all. Marriage would have been disastrous." Valan flashed a grin. "The passion of youth." Gordon's eyes sparked. Valan gave him no chance to reply, but turned to Lady Chastity. "Might I impose upon you, my lady, to take Miss Matheson home with you tonight—with your husband's permission, of course? Tomorrow, my ward will have a female companion at Finley Hall."

"I would be pleased to have Miss Matheson stay with us," she replied.

Valan addressed Miss Matheson. "Would you prefer to stay with Lady Chastity rather than return to Lady Peddington's school?"

She beamed. "Oh, indeed, I would, sir."

He smiled. "Good, then go with her, as I ask."

She pinned him with a shrewd look. "Promise that tomorrow you will find a companion for me and I shall come live with you?"

"You must save your penchant for negotiation for business," he said.

"That is not an answer," she said.

He sighed. "I promise, my child."

She wrinkled her nose. "And you will stop calling me 'child.'"

He angled his head with cultured grace. "As you command."

She gave a succinct nod. "Then I shall do as you ask." She looked at Lady Chastity. "I will leave when you are ready."

Lady Chastity exchanged a look with her husband, then said, "We can leave now."

"My lord," Gordon said to Sir Stirling, "surely you see how dangerous this situation is for Miss Matheson?"

Sir Stirling's expression chilled. "In fact, there is nowhere safer for her than in the company of my wife."

Gordon paled. "Of course. That is not what I meant. I only meant that Northington's plans for her are less than honorable."

Miss Matheson snorted. "I am done with this one. We may go."

Valan regarded her severely. "I beg of you, Miss Matheson, do not snort like a common tavern wench."

She hung her head. "I am sorry, sir."

"You are forgiven. Now, go with Lady Chastity and, I beg you, behave—at least until I next see you."

"I promise." She gave him a full smile before he said to Sir Stirling, "Good evening, Sir Stirling." He faced Lady Chastity. "My lady, thank you for your kindness."

Without so much as a glance at Gordon, he strode away.

FINDING A GOVERNESS ON SHORT NOTICE WASN'T TERRIBLY HARD. Finding one who would not crumble under Miss Matheson's determined nature, proved more difficult. Valan settled for a woman of twenty-eight years, who was taller than his new ward by at least five inches. One would think her height would give her an advantage, but her light brown hair fastened in a severe chignon, combined with her quiet manner, reminded him of a sparrow.

She sat across from him in the carriage, her hands folded demurely in her lap, as befitted a paid companion. For today, she would satisfy propriety. He would hire someone more suitable post haste.

They reached Stirling's home exactly at four p.m., as Valan had promised in his note sent earlier that day. He alighted from the coach, then turned and assisted Miss Stone to the ground. They proceeded up the walkway and up the three steps to the door.

He knocked. A moment later, the door opened, and an austere butler led them down a short hallway and into a parlor, tastefully decorated in pale gold and blues.

"I shall tell his lordship you are here." He bowed and left.

Thankfully, Miss Stone remained quiet while they waited.

Minutes later, Sir Stirling and Lady Chastity entered with Miss Matheson between them. Miss Matheson flew across the room and threw herself into Valan's arms.

"I am so pleased to see you, sir."

"So I gather." He grasped her shoulders and set her at arm's length. "Our first order of business when we arrive home will be a serious discussion on your conduct with a gentleman." Valan turned and bowed to Lady Chastity. "My lady. You are looking particularly radiant." She cast a curious glance at her husband. Valan turned to Sir Stirling. "Your lordship. May I introduce Miss Stone. Miss Stone, the Marquess and Marchioness of Roxburgh."

Miss Stone curtsied.

He nodded toward Jeanine. "This is your charge, Miss Matheson."

"I am not her charge," Miss Matheson said. "We agreed that I am not a child."

"I believe I agreed not to *call* you a child," Valan said.

Miss Matheson cast him a sideways glance, then said to Miss Stone, "You are very tall."

"That is not polite," Valan said. "I wager Miss Peddington taught you better manners."

"I did not say being tall was a bad thing. So, I wasn't being rude."

"Perhaps we do not understand one another," he said. "If you want to be my ward, you will not contradict me."

"I—"

"Do you wish to be my ward?" he cut in.

She clamped her mouth shut and nodded.

"Then we are agreed," he said.

She nodded again and looked at Miss Stone. "Truly, I meant no offense."

The young woman smiled. "It is true, I am unusually tall, but I'm certain I surprised you. His lordship is correct, however. A lady never points out another's shortcomings, no matter how obvious they are."

Miss Matheson's eyes darkened. "Being tall is not a shortcoming. Anyone who says otherwise is cruel."

"You are right, of course," Miss Stone said.

Miss Matheson's expression cleared. "We shall get along famously." She looked up at Valan and smiled. "You have chosen well, sir.

He lifted a brow. "Have I, indeed?"

"You have, and are quite pleased with yourself."

"A man takes pleasure where he can. Shall we go?"

"May I have a word with you before you leave?" Stirling said.

Valan angled his head in agreement, then said to Miss Matheson, "Will you and Miss Stone wait in the carriage, please?"

"Come along, ladies," Lady Chastity said. "We will make certain Miss Matheson's boxes are collected."

"Boxes?" Valan repeated.

"Chastity purchased a few essentials for Miss Matheson," Sir Stirling said.

"How kind of you," Valan said.

The ladies left, and Valan said, "Thank you for keeping her. Please forward me the bills for her things."

Stirling shook his head. "Chastity wanted to give her a few items. I promise you, the real expense for her wardrobe still lays with you. She's a very vivacious young lady."

Valan met his gaze squarely. "I have no designs on her, if that is your concern."

"I'm not the least bit concerned. I thought you might like to know that Lord Gordon has petitioned Chastity's father to intercede for the girl."

"Has he, now?" Valan murmured. "One wonders where Lord Gordon finds the time to crusade so determinedly. His own father's affairs have suffered these last two years."

"He has designs on her, of course," Stirling said.

Valan stared. "I had no idea you were so forthright."

Sterling laughed. "I'm not always. But I feel certain you already knew Gordon wanted her."

"Aye," Valan said. "I haven't known him to do anything out of the goodness of his heart."

"Many would say the same of you," Sterling said.

"They would be right," Valan admitted.

"Then why do this?"

"Whatever my reasons, I do not lie when I say the girl is in no danger from me."

Stirling studied him. "Those reasons are, I think, to annoy Lord Gordon."

"I'm not certain I believe you when you say you're not always so forthright," Valan said.

Stirling smiled. "Nonetheless, it is true. Being blunt with you is necessary."

"I see," Valan said in a dry voice. "Will His Grace interfere?"

Stirling shook his head. "I doubt it. Chastity will speak with him."

"I'm surprised she isn't concerned for Miss Matheson," Valan said.

Stirling's grin widened. "Chastity married a man who carried her down the aisle over his shoulder then *encouraged* her to take her vows. She is not given to nerves, particularly around unorthodox men."

"You are a fortunate man."

"I am. If ye need further help, don't hesitate to ask," Stirling said.

Valan thanked him, took his leave, and found his ward and her chaperone waiting in the carriage, boxes piled high on top of the vehicle.

Miss Matheson squealed with delight as he stepped into the carriage and pulled the door shut. Valan sat on the seat opposite them. "Miss Matheson, I ask that you conduct yourself as purports a lady. You will notice that Miss Stone remained calm as I entered the carriage. Please follow her example."

"You cannot expect all ladies to react in exactly the same fashion, sir."

Valan rapped on the roof of the carriage, which soon jolted into motion. "In public, and in matters of propriety, I can, indeed, expect you to adhere to similar manners."

She tilted her head. "But in private, I may behave naturally?"

"You may speak plainly with me, Miss Matheson."

She made a face.

He sighed. "What is it now?"

"If we are to speak plainly when alone, then you must call me Jennie."

"I will not," he said. "Jeanine, will do."

"My mother and sisters call me Jennie," she said.

"That is their prerogative," he said. "In public, or when we have guests, I will call you Miss Matheson. When we are at home or alone, I will call you Jeanine."

She clapped her hands. "And I shall call you Valan."

He shook his head. "In public, you will address me as 'my lord' or 'Lord Northington,' or even 'sir.' In private, you will address me as 'sir' or 'my lord.'"

She wrinkled her nose. "It does not seem fair that you can call me by my Christian name, but I must always call you 'my lord' or 'sir.'"

"Anyone who told you life is fair, my dear, was lying."

CHAPTER 4

THEY ARRIVED HOME TO FIND TEA WAITING FOR THEM IN THE parlor.

Jeanine and Miss Matheson settled on the settee and Valan took the chair to their left. Miss Stone poured and handed out the cups.

"What does a ward do?" Jeanine asked.

Valan paused as he lifted the teacup to his lips. "I am not quite sure."

"She will continue her education as a lady," Miss Stone said. "Sewing, pianoforte, party planning, perhaps a little Latin and French. *Parlez-vous françaiss, mademoiselle?*" she said in flawless French.

"Miss Stone, you surprise me," Valan said.

"*Tu parles français comme un parisien,*" Jeanine said.

"Miss Matheson," Valan said in delight. "You, too, speak French like a Parisian. Where did you learn?"

"From Lady Peddington, of course."

"Surely, you spoke the language before you attended her school," he said.

Jeanine beamed and shook her head. "Nae. She said I was a

natural. I don't speak fluently, but I would love to visit Paris and practice."

"Well, the way you and Miss Stone speak French, it would be a crime not to go." He looked at Miss Stone. "Is a trip to France permissible for a ward?"

"Very much so, sir."

"Then it's settled."

Baldwin entered, carrying a single envelope on a silver tray. "Forgive the interruption, my lord." He stopped in front of Valan. "This just arrived for you from Lady Douglas. Her man awaits a reply."

Valan set down his teacup, took the envelope and pulled the notecard from within:

An invitation from Lady Douglas for an intimate luncheon on the morrow. He looked at Baldwin. "Please have the man waiting, inform Lady Douglas that Miss Matheson and Miss Stone will be happy to attend the party."

"As you wish, sir." Baldwin bowed and left.

"A party?" Miss Matheson said.

Valan handed her the invitation.

She scanned the note, then looked up. "How did Lady Douglas learn so soon that I am to be your ward?"

"You are not 'to be' my ward," Valan corrected. "You *are* my ward. As for how she knew so quickly…" He thought of Lord Gordon. "*Society* always finds a way to spread the latest news."

"I am not particularly interested in a luncheon," Jeanine said.

"Miss Douglas has been kind enough to extend the invitation at this late date. You will attend."

"You do not mean to attend?" she demanded.

He hadn't planned to attend, then imagined her strolling in the garden and being accosted by a wolf who didn't know she was the Marquess of Northington's ward. "Of course, I will accompany you."

Mischief danced in her eyes. "You're afraid to let me go alone, aren't you?"

"I fear, whether I accompany you or not, we shall have our challenges."

"We must bring Miss Stone, of course."

"Of course. Anywhere you go, Miss Stone goes."

The lady looked startled. "Forgive me, my lord, but I do not have a gown for such grand parties."

"Hmm." He looked at Jeanine. "May I ask how many gowns you own?"

"Three ball gowns and one day dress."

"Just as I thought." Valan glanced at the mantle clock. 5:45.

He rose and crossed to the small secretary located near the hearth. He jotted a note to the modiste, then tugged the bell pull. Baldwin appeared before he'd returned to his seat.

"Baldwin, please have this note sent to Mrs. Morgan. She lives on the end of Bryant Street, a modest brick building, if I recall. Wait for a reply. If she is able to come now, please fetch her." He handed the note to the steward.

Baldwin bowed, then left.

"I don't see why you must buy new gowns," Jeanine said.

Valan returned to his chair. "Would you rob Miss Stone of the pleasure of new gowns?"

"Oh, you're right, of course."

"Of course." Valan reached for his tea, then decided something stronger was called for. He went to the sideboard, and poured a liberal dose of scotch into a glass tumbler.

"You need not trouble yourself on my account, sir," said Miss Stone.

Valan returned to his seat, swirled the liquor and took a sniff before drinking half the liquid. He looked at her and smiled politely. "As I will not sew the dresses, it is no trouble for me."

"But the expense," Miss Stone said.

Valan regarded them. "I wonder at my good fortune to find the only two women in Scotland who care nothing for new dresses."

"No one said we didn't care," Jeanine said. "But, really, how many dresses does a woman need?"

"How many, indeed?" he repeated softly.

Jeanine started to open the library door, then paused and knocked.

"Enter," the marquess called.

She opened the door. Despite the gloomy weather, the red of the wall paint and deep blues of the curtains gave the room a warm feel. To her left, French doors paned with glass stood open to reveal a quaint balcony. Opposite the balcony doors, books filled ceiling-high cherrywood shelves. A rolling ladder leaned against the shelves to the right of the marquess's desk, where he sat, a quill in hand. He'd paused his letter writing to watch her.

She smiled. "I like this room."

"I am deeply gratified." His attention returned to his letter. "To what do I owe the honor of your visit this morning?"

"Visit? We live in the same house."

"In this large house, it is conceivable that we might not see one another for weeks."

"Weeks?" She crossed to the chair opposite his desk and sat down. "That is terrible. I will see you every day."

"How fortunate for me," he said dryly.

"You do not wish to see me?"

"I am always pleased to see you," he said. "But I expect you will be busy, what with today's party and your lessons in Latin and French, sewing, shopping and dress fittings—" he spared her a glance "—I assume you have more fittings?"

"Miss Stone insisted."

He nodded and resumed writing. "Have you and Miss Stone reviewed the latest party invitations?"

She scrunched her nose in distaste. "Can't I simply pick one from the pile? They're all the same."

"Forgive me, but they're not all the same."

She waved an airy hand. "Dancing, champagne, crowded ballrooms, pheasant for dinner—they are alike."

With a sigh, he laid down his pen and leaned back in his chair. "Perhaps there are some similarities in the programming, but I can assure you, that does not mean they are all the same."

"You mean that some are more socially important than others."

He nodded. "Something you might remember, if you are to find that elderly gentleman you want."

"How long do you think it will take me to find this gentleman?"

"Are you in a hurry?" he asked.

"I will no' be young forever," she said. "I am already nineteen."

He nodded gravely, but the glint in his eyes told her he was laughing at her. "I believe you have enough time to find someone before you are on the shelf."

"Laugh all you want," she said. "There are plenty of younger women than I—and more beautiful. I cannot afford to waste time. My younger sisters are already married."

He regarded her. "You are bothered by the fact that they married before you?"

"Of course. The eldest sister is supposed to marry first."

"Surely, there was some young man you could have married?"

"There are always young men to marry. But I want a wealthy gentleman who…"

"Who is ready to move on to his reward?" he finished for her. "This has been a plan of yours for some time, I take it?"

Jeanine nodded. "Since my mother decided to remarry, two years ago. They only just married last year, which is why I knew I had to take action."

His lordships' brows shot up in surprise. "You have a father?"

"Stepfather," she corrected. "It isn't at all the same thing."

"Either way, he will have something to say about who you marry," the marquess said. "Surely, he will want you to return home and find a husband?"

"Oh no, I can never return home." Her gaze caught on the small game table to the left of the ladder. "Is that a chess board?"

"There is a chess board inside the table," he said.

"I like chess. Will you play with me sometime?"

"If you like. Why can you never return home?" he asked." His eyes shifted past Jeanine and she twisted in her chair as a light knock came to the open door. Miss Stone stood in the doorway.

"Come in," his lordship said.

Jeanine jumped to her feet as Miss Stone approached. "Doesn't she look lovely? The pale yellow fabric compliments her complexion. The needlework on the ruffled sleeves is perfect. I insisted that Mrs. Morgan sew her a day dress straight away. It arrived last night."

His eyes bore into Miss Stone. "And she agreed?" he said.

Miss Stone stopped in front of his desk. "Nae, sir, I did not. In fact, I instructed Mrs. Morgan to sew Miss Matheson's dress first. When this dress arrived yesterday, I sent her a note demanding to know why she had ignored my instructions."

The marquess's eyes shifted to Jeanine. "I have an idea why."

"Do not be angry," Jeanine said. "You must agree that Miss Stone's clothes are...oh, what is the word, outdated—yes—

that's it, her clothes are outdated. Whereas, mine are only not as lavish as you would like."

"I would not have even worn the dress, my lord," Miss Stone said, "but Miss Matheson threatened to burn my clothes if I didn't."

"She is quite capable of carrying out the threat," he murmured.

Miss Stone clasped her hands at her waist." Forgive me for saying so, sir, but I believe she is."

"Perhaps that is the threat I should use against her clothes," he said.

"I doubt it would work, sir," Miss Stone said. "She would only devise a way to get even."

His lordship's brows shot up. "You surprise me, Miss Stone."

"I cannot imagine why, my lord."

"You comprehend Miss Matheson's character better than I thought you would."

"It isn't hard. She does little to hide her actions and motivations."

He looked at Jeanine and she grinned. "Nae, she does not," he said.

Miss Stone turned to Jeanine. "We must leave in half an hour, if we are to arrive at Mrs. Morgan's shop on time."

"Just as I thought." The marquess picked up his quill. "I will meet you ladies in the foyer at two-thirty."

"I won't see you until then?" Jeanine asked.

"I did say I expected that you would be busy today, Miss Matheson."

She lifted a finger. "You promised to call me Jeanine in the privacy of our home."

A corner of his mouth twitched. "In the privacy of *our* home. Aye, Jeanine."

She smiled. "Very good, Valan."

His gaze sharpened. "I also said, you would address me as either 'sir' or 'my lord.'"

"Aye, that is what you said," she replied, then turned, and left with Miss Stone.

~

At the luncheon, the marquess allowed Jeanine to have two glasses of wine—well, technically, one glass, for each time he filled the glass only halfway. She now watched as he played commerce with three other gentlemen near the balcony, at a table in a corner of the massive parlor. A servant appeared at the table and filled the men's glasses with sherry and brandy, then left.

"Ye might bring some scotch, lad," said the large gentleman to the marquess's right.

"The French brandy isn't good enough for you?" Mr. Phillips said.

"Brandy is well and good," he said in a thick Scottish burr, "but a man needs strong liquor when he's gambling."

"This is not a hell, MacLean," Phillips said.

The man grinned. "Depends on if ye are winning or losing."

Jeanine glanced at the refreshments table on the far side of the room. Half a dozen people gathered around the table. Perhaps she could nip over and fill her wine glass without being missed.

"Where is Miss Stone, Miss Matheson?" his lordship asked.

Jeanine started. "Lady Douglas has taken her away."

"Away?" He glanced at her.

"Aye," she replied. "I believe Lady Douglas wanted to learn more about Miss Stone's previous employer."

In the instant before he returned his gaze to his cards, she glimpsed a strange smile. From the corner of her eye, a flash of red captured her attention. She turned slightly and recognized

Lord Gordon as he entered the room. His bright burgundy coat made him stand out like a parrot amongst sparrows. He passed from sight behind a group of men.

He did not approve of her being the ward of the Marquess of Northington—which was foolish. Anyone with eyes could see the marquess hadn't taken her as ward in order to make her his lover.

"Miss Matheson," the marquess said, "sit. I will teach you how to play commerce."

"Really?" Jeanine cried. "I would love to play."

He stood and stepped around his chair. "Have my seat." She took the chair. He pushed it closer to the table, then signaled a servant to bring another chair.

The Scot sitting to her right, stood. "No need to call for another chair, Northington. You took my last hundred pounds. I'm out. Take my chair."

His lordship gave a slight bow. "Thank you, MacLean." He sat down, then scooted his chair closer to hers. "Phillips," he nodded to the dealer, who sat directly across from them, "I will sit out this round. Please deal the lady in."

"Perhaps the lady would prefer a game of vingt-et-un," the handsome gentleman to her left said.

Jeanine started to roll her eyes, then caught sight of the marquess's arched brows. She peeked at him from beneath her lashes and then looked at the gentleman and smiled sweetly. "If you are more comfortable with a game of luck, sir, I will oblige."

Chuckles sounded behind her.

"Miss Matheson may play commerce if she chooses," the marquess said. "I promised to teach her."

The man looked back at Jeanine and angled his head. "As you wish, ma'am."

"The object of the game," the marquess began.

"Oh, I know the game," Jeanine said.

"Indeed?" he said. "You didn't tell me you know how to play."

"You didn't ask," she replied as Phillips began the deal.

"She's got you there, Northington," a man said behind her.

Phillips laid three cards facedown before each of the four players, himself included, then laid three cards face up to form the widow. An ace of hearts, two of clubs, and ten of diamonds. He placed a fifty pound note in the middle of the table. The other two men did the same, and the marquess took a fifty pound note from the stack of bills in front of him and tossed it onto the pile.

Phillips took the ace, slipped it facedown at the bottom of his three cards, then took his top facedown card and turned it up beside the other two face-up cards. A murmur went up. He'd exchanged the ace of hearts for a king of hearts. He would be wanting that card back.

Jeanine lifted the corners of her three cards and looked at them. Three of spades, queen of clubs, and an ace of diamonds. The marquess leaned toward her.

Jeanine covered her cards and looked at him. "What are you doing?"

"I am not playing," he said. "It is permissible to show me your cards."

She shook her head. "I don't want your expression to give away my hand."

More chuckles from the men.

His lordship lifted a brow. "Are you saying I cannot school my expression?"

"Would you let me see your cards if you were playing?" she asked.

"It is only fair I see how you are spending my money," he countered.

Jeanine started to snort, then thought better of it. "I am not spending it," she replied. "It is simply a stake."

The blond gentleman to Phillips' left traded a four of diamonds for the king Phillips had discarded. Good. It was unlikely Phillips would be able to get the king now.

Jeanine traded her queen for the two of clubs. The handsome gentleman to her left took her queen and left the four of spades. The round had reached Phillips, and he pulled another card from the deck and laid it face up with the widow. A Jack of spades. Phillips placed another fifty-pound note in the pool. The player to his left shook his head and leaned back in his chair. Janine reached for a hundred-pound note in the stack in front of the marquess.

He placed a staying hand on hers. "Perhaps you should show me your cards, Miss Matheson."

"That would ruin the game," she said. "If you approve the bet, no one will match me, and I won't win as much money." He didn't move and she added, "If I lose, you will lose less than the cost of that waistcoat."

His expression remained impassive. "I believe you already owe me the cost of one waistcoat."

"All the more reason for me to make the bet."

He remained motionless for two heartbeats, then removed his hand. She took the hundred-pound note and added it to the pool.

The handsome gentleman to her left placed a hundred pound note on top of hers. "I pray you will not hold it against me if I am the man responsible for you owing Lord Northington the price of two waistcoats."

She shrugged. "Since I will win, that will not be an issue."

The bet returned to Phillips. His mouth thinned, but he added another fifty-pound note, then traded the jack he'd just laid down for a six of clubs. The play was now Jeanine's and, with a smile, she gave a small shake of her head. Two more rounds followed before the handsome gentleman picked up a nine and discarded a two. Her gaze snagged on the card and, as hoped, when Phillips added a new card to the widow, a three of diamonds, he exchanged a seven for the two.

Jeanine relaxed against her chair, intensely aware of his lordship's eyes on her. When her turn came, she looked at the marquess, smiled, then took another hundred-pound note from his stack and added it to the pool. Phillips visibly blanched. The handsome gentleman matched her bet, but took no cards.

Phillips' gaze locked with hers. "As you can see, Miss Matheson, I do not have the money to match your bet. I assume you will take my marker." He reached into his coat pocket.

Jeanine shook her head. "Nae, sir, I do not accept bets from men who can't afford to lose their money."

His face reddened. "You mistake the lack of money on my person for an inability to pay."

She shrugged. "Then next time, bring more money."

Phillips opened his mouth to reply, but the marquess said, "It is the other player's prerogative to decline a marker, Phillips."

"She is only declining my marker because she knows that will eliminate me from the game," he snapped.

"That is a strategy that will likely save you a great deal of money this night," his lordship replied, then said to Jeanine, "It is your turn, Miss Matheson."

She reached for the marquess's pile of money. This time, he didn't stop her when she placed five hundred-pound notes in the pool. Jeanine met the handsome gentleman's gaze.

He angled his head slightly. "I will forfeit the bet to you."

"Of course, you will." She laughed. "You do not have the money to match my bet."

"Perhaps not," he said. "Show us your cards."

She shook her head and laughed again. "You did not pay for the privilege of seeing my cards."

"True," he agreed. "But I ask it as a favor."

Jeanine shrugged, then turned over her cards.

Laughter and murmurs rose amongst the men.

"Beat by an ace, two and three," the handsome gentleman said. "You are a very good player, Miss Matheson. May I ask where you learned to play?"

"I have six cousins, all boys. They taught me."

"By all that is holy, Northington, you are letting her gamble?"

Jeanine turned slightly and looked up at Lord Gordon. The burgundy coat really was horrid.

"Why not?" the handsome gentleman said. "Such talent shouldn't go to waste."

"This is exactly what I feared," Lord Gordon said.

"I was certain it was something else you feared, my dear," the marquess drawled.

Lord Gordon pointedly ignored him. "Miss Matheson, would you care to have a glass of punch with me?"

The handsome gentleman stood. "You are too late, Gordon. The lady has agreed to take a turn around the room with me." He looked at the marquess. "With your permission, of course, my lord."

His attention shifted to the handsome gentleman. "You will not leave the parlor."

"Of course not." The handsome gentleman smiled at her.

She would have refused, but remembered the refreshments table on the other side of the room. An escort would be nice, not to mention, the marquess was likely not to let her go too far out of his sight alone. She rose, and the other men stood as the marquess pulled her chair out for her.

Jeanine faced the handsome gentleman. "Oh, dear, I don't know your name."

"That is my fault," his lordship said.

"You are going to allow Miss Matheson to-to *go off* with a man she hasn't been introduced to?" Lord Gordon cried.

"I don't think it's as bad as all that," Lord Northington said. "A turn around the room isn't 'going off' with someone. And I was about to introduce her to Mr. Westland. Mr. Westland, may I introduce my ward, Miss Matheson."

Mr. Westland grasped her hand and bent over her fingers. "An honor to meet you, Miss Matheson."

"You're not angry that I beat you at cards?" she asked. "My cousins would get so angry when I beat them, they wouldn't play with me for weeks. Eventually, they would need another player and be forced to ask me to play."

Mr. Westland smiled. "I am not at all angry."

She smiled. "Good. Otherwise, it would be awkward for us to walk together."

"Indeed," he said with a laugh, then extended an arm. Jeanine laid her hand atop his as they started away, and behind her Lord Gordon said, "I must protest."

"At least he didn't protest while pointing a pistol," Phillips mumbled.

The table went dead silent and Jeanine glanced over her shoulder.

His lordship stared at Mr. Phillips, a strange smile playing on his lips.

"Didn't mean anything by it," Phillips said.

"Oh, but you did," the marquess said.

Jeanine faced forward.

"I will be speaking with His Grace about this," she heard Lord Gordon say.

"Of course, you will," his lordship said before she passed beyond hearing.

CHAPTER 5

VALAN DID NOT THROW PARTIES. BUT THEN, HE'D NEVER BEFORE had a ward.

He spent the week out and about to ensure everyone knew about the upcoming party, whether they were invited or not. The spare moments of respite away from his once quiet household were spent at his club, where no one spoke above a murmur, even on days like today, when seats were in high demand.

Valan read his newspaper in the quiet corner hear the hearth, but noted the approach of Baron Rosemund, who claimed an empty chair at the small round table to Valan's right.

"Kind of you to have brandy ready for me." Brendan reached across the intervening space, lifted Valan's decanter and filled the empty glass that sat beside Valan's full glass.

"I regret to tell you, that the brandy was not for you," Valan replied.

"I am wounded." Brendan set the decanter down, picked up the filled glass, relaxed against his chair and rested the glass on his leg. "You are making quite a stir these days. Tell me the latest gossip isn't true."

Valan perused the business section of the paper. "At the risk of sounding pompous, which latest gossip do you mean?"

Brendan gave him a sideways glance.

"Aye, it is true," Valan said.

Brendan sipped his brandy. "Is she beautiful?"

"Some would say so."

"That is a new tack for you."

"She is my ward," Valan said.

"I know you too well to believe this isn't something more," Brendan said without rancor.

Valan chuckled. "You bear quite a burden being my friend."

"A thankless task," he replied with wry humor.

Valan lowered his newspaper and looked at him. "I beg your pardon, that was a fine dinner we enjoyed last month in Inverness—at my expense."

Brendan lifted his glass in salute. "Many thanks." He took another sip. "If you don't have designs on the woman, what could possibly induce you to take her as your ward?"

Twenty years dropped away, as Valan once again fitted his booted foot to the final rung in the trestle leading to Lady Victoria's bedchamber window and grasped the window sill. He hoisted himself up and swung his feet over, then straightened in the dimly lit room. It wasn't the cool metal of the pistol pressed to the back of his neck when he stepped deeper inside the room that bothered him—if he had an undcrage sister and a man had climbed through her window, he would've done the same—but the pistol Gordon held when he emerged from the dressing screen across the room.

Despite prolonged efforts, Valan never learned how Gordon had discovered that Valan's father had shot himself only hours before, leaving Valan a pauper. The only thing his father hadn't lost in that card game was their ancestral castle on the Isle of Mull. Valan hadn't visited the castle since.

As if on cue, Lord Gordon entered the sitting room. Valan reached for his glass of brandy and directed his attention back to the paper. Three heartbeats later, Lord Gordon entered his peripheral view. An instant later, he stopped in front of him. Valan kept his attention on his paper.

"Rosemund," Gordon said with a curt nod to Brendan, then to Valan, "A word with you, Northington."

Valan kept his gaze on the paper. "Of course."

"In private, if you will."

"I have no secrets from Brendan. Say what you will."

A moment of silence passed, then Gordon said, "At least do me the courtesy of giving me your full attention."

Valan lifted his gaze from the paper. "Forgive me. Will you sit? I can call for a chair and another brandy glass."

"You can call for— I can have a chair brought, if I so choose," he snapped. "I do not need you to command one of your lackeys."

"I would hardly call Brummell's servants 'lackeys,' and they are not my lackey's, at any rate." He sipped his brandy, then stared, waiting.

Gordon drew himself up as if for battle. "I have appealed to Duke Roxburgh to intervene on Miss Matheson's behalf."

"I expected nothing less. Pray, sit. I am distressed that you stand while we sit."

"I am satisfied to stand," he said. "I demand you return Miss Matheson to Lady Peddington's school."

"Return her? You speak as if she is property. You credit me with far too much influence. First, Brummell's servants are my lackeys, now I own Miss Matheson. I admit that a lady has her pleasant uses, but I am enlightened enough to know that I do not own a single one." He thought of Jeanine's desire to marry a wealthy old gentleman with one foot in the grave. That young lady had no intention of ever becoming property.

"You know full well the child has no comprehension of your intentions," Lord Gordon said. "She sees you only as a generous benefactor."

Valan smiled. "An intelligent female, to be sure."

"An innocent in the clutches of a man who charms women for nefarious purposes," Lord Gordon snapped.

"I am indeed guilty of that. But perhaps not in this case."

"I am giving you the opportunity to do the right thing before it is too late," Lord Gordon said.

Valan laughed. "You never cease to amuse. You, of all people, know it is far too late for me to do the right thing."

"I warn you," Gordon said through tight lips.

"You are overset, my dear," Valan said. "A brandy would do you good. Are you sure—"

"Nae, I do not want a damned brandy," Gordon nearly shouted.

Glances came their way. Gordon sent a withering glare to a man seated at a nearby table, then whirled and stalked from the room.

"I believe you," Brendan said.

Valan looked at him. "I am gratified to have your trust, but to what do I own such an honor?"

"Your ward--what is her name...Miss Matheson--is safe from your masculine clutches."

"I have many faults," Valan said, "but lying is not one of them."

"You simply say nothing," Brendon said.

Valan shrugged.

"It's been twenty years," Brendon said. "I thought you'd forgotten."

Valan offered a wistful smile. "Then, Brendan, you don't know me as well as you thought you did."

Valan entered his library and went straight to the sideboard to pour himself a brandy.

"There you are."

He glanced right as Miss Matheson hurried into the room with Miss Stone following at a sedate pace.

He replaced the decanter's top, crossed to his desk, and sat down. "Good afternoon, Miss Matheson. Miss Stone."

Miss Stone halted before his desk, hands clasped in front of her.

Jeanine sat in the chair opposite his desk, then jumped to her feet. "We need a chair for you, Miss Stone."

"I am content to stand," she said.

Jeanine's eyes lit on the chairs that surrounded the gaming table.

Valan rose. "Sit, Jeanine. I will fetch the chair."

She smiled. "You are gallant."

"Hardly," he replied. "I fear you will topple and break your neck if you try to carry the chair." He carried the chair to the desk and set it to her left. "Miss Stone, you may sit."

She obeyed and he returned to his seat. "Do you need something?" he asked.

"We don't need anything," Jeanine said. "Well, unless you count answering a question as needing something."

"Ask the question and we shall see." He sipped his brandy.

"Are we allowed to invite guests to the party?"

"Who are the guests?"

"My friends from Lady Peddington's school."

"Aye," he replied. "You may invite them."

She beamed. "See, that wasn't so difficult, now, was it?"

"It was not."

"Have you invited everyone you wanted to invite?" she asked.

"For the most part."

"Who have you invited?"

"I doubt you know most of them." He paused in lifting the glass to his lips. "Where are you from?"

She giggled. "How funny that you made me your ward and you never asked where I lived."

"I believe I did ask you that night at Lady Peddington's ball, but you wouldn't tell me." he said, and drank half the brandy.

"You're right, of course." Jeanine regarded him. "Why did you make me your ward?"

"It is polite to answer the question you were asked before you ask one," he said.

Her eyes twinkled. "I am from Perth. Now, why did you make me your ward?"

"To aid in your quest to find a husband."

"That is silly." She looked at Miss Stone. "Isn't that silly, Miss Stone?"

"You are fortunate that his lordship has taken an interest in your well-being," she replied.

Jeanine waved a hand. "Oh, I know that. But that doesn't change the fact that he didn't have to take an interest. What kind of food will there be at the party? Please don't say pheasant. Everyone serves pheasant."

"I have no idea what is on the menu. You may speak with Mrs. McPhee, if you wish."

"Will there be dancing?"

He nodded. "Aye."

"I love to dance. You can dance with me—and Miss Stone, as well."

"There will be many young bucks anxious to dance with you and Miss Stone."

She shook her head. "Miss Stone may dance with them, of course. But you know I am not interested in a young buck."

His mouth twitched. "You would rob them of the pleasure of your company?"

She snorted. "They do not care about my company."

"Mr. Westland seemed to enjoy your company at the luncheon. Did you not find him charming?"

"He is charming." She cast a sideways glance at Miss Stone. "He would enjoy Miss Stone's company much more, however."

"I could never replace you," Miss Stone said.

"Of course, you could," Jeanine said. "Did you notice Miss Stone's hair, Grey? It is my creation. She is lovely, isn't she?"

He started. "What did you call me?"

She smiled. "Grey."

"I believe I said that you were to address me as 'sir' or 'my lord.'"

"You did, but when we are alone, that is too formal for a family."

He lifted a brow. "Family?"

She nodded enthusiastically.

"We are not alone," he pointed out. "Miss Stone is present."

"Isn't Miss Stone a part of our family?" Jeanine asked.

"I suppose she is." Valan lifted his glass to Miss Stone. "My condolences, Miss Stone." He finished the sherry and started to rise, then paused when Baldwin entered.

"Pardon the interruption, my lord, but there is a problem with a delivery."

Valan frowned. "What can that possibly have to do with me?"

"Mrs. McPhee is arguing with the deliveryman and I fear they will come to blows."

"If that happens, then we must pity the deliveryman. What is the argument?"

"Mrs. McPhee insists the delivery is too much. The deliveryman swears that this is the amount ordered for the party."

"You are the steward," Valan said. "Deal with the matter."

Mrs. MacPhee's voice rose in the hallway. A man's muffled reply followed.

Valan pinned Baldwin with a horrified stare. "Is a deliveryman actually headed for my study?"

"He is quite determined, my lord," Baldwin said.

The voices neared, and Mrs. McPhee burst into the room with a short, stalky man close on her heels. He appeared small beside her stout frame.

"There ye are, my lord." Mrs. McPhee hurried to his desk and halted near Miss Stone's chair.

The deliveryman stopped beside her.

"I have had enough of this miscreant," the housekeeper said.

"I am no miscreant," the man growled. "I only want to be paid for my delivery."

She narrowed her eyes on him. "I will not pay for something I didn't order."

The deliveryman shook a piece of paper in her face. "I cannae sell the fresh vegetables anywhere else. They will rot."

"That is *your* mistake," she said.

The man opened his mouth to rebut, but Valan stood and said, "May I ask who ordered the, er, vegetables, is it?"

The man thrust his paper toward Valan. Valan took it and scanned the list. He looked at Mrs. McPhee. "Who wrote the list?"

"That is Brenda's handwriting."

"Brenda?" Valan searched his memory. "She assists in the kitchen?"

Mrs. McPhee nodded.

"Then you did order the vegetables," he said.

She shook her head. "If ye look at the amounts, they have been scratched out and larger portions written in. This man is trying to cheat us."

"I never cheated anyone in my life," the deliveryman burst out.

Valan looked at the list again. "Is this the first order of vegetables for the party?"

"It is," replied Mrs. McPhee.

"In fact, it doesn't seem to be enough for the two hundred and fifty guests we invited," he said. "I expect at least fifty more spouses and friends to accompany the invited guests."

"I told ye that you needed more," the delivery man interjected.

"I will not buy more vegetables until I am sure we need more," Mrs. McPhee shot back. "His lordship doesn't like to waste money."

"While I appreciate your consideration, Mrs. McPhee, I do, in fact, waste money, and quite often," Valan said. "This does not seem to me an exorbitant amount to spend on vegetables."

"We cannae trust a man who tries to bilk us," she insisted.

The man swung to face her squarely and was forced to look up at her. "I willnae have my honor called into question."

"Honor?" she cried. "Thieves have no honor."

The man stepped closer. Mrs. McPhee drew back a fist and drove it into his jaw. He jerked left. Valan glimpsed Miss Stone's slippered foot shoot out right before the man tripped over her foot and flailed backwards two steps. Jeanine leapt to her feet. The deliveryman crashed into the game table. Wood splintered and game pieces flew everywhere. Valan took three steps and stopped beside him.

"He's broken your table," Jeanine cried.

"So he has."

The man sat up and gave his head a shake. He started to push to his feet.

"I suggest you stay down," Valan said. "Mrs. McPhee outweighs you by at least two stone."

The man looked up at him and blinked. "What?"

"As you may have guessed, Mrs. McPhee does not back down from a fight," Valan said.

The man's dazed eyes slipped past him. His face reddened and he struggled to his feet. "I demand my money."

"Why you scoundrel," Mrs. McPhee muttered darkly.

"Baldwin," Valan said, "pay the gentleman and see him safely out the door."

The deliveryman kept his glare fixed on Mrs. McPhee, who deigned to cast only a cursory glance at him as he passed. Valan looked at his game table and sighed before returning to his seat. Miss Stone, he noted, sat primly in her seat, hands clasped on her lap.

"Mrs. McPhee," Jeanine said a little breathless, "I have never seen anything so courageous. How did you manage to hit him so hard? Doesn't your hand hurt? I once punched Willy, my oldest cousin, and my hand hurt for days."

"I use my right hand to pound bread dough," the housekeeper replied with pride. "My right hand is stronger than the left."

"Perhaps I should start pounding bread dough," Jeanine said.

"Not if you intend to punch someone," Valan said.

Mrs. McPhee drew herself up. "The man deserved everything I gave him."

"A man almost always deserves what a woman gives him," Valan said. "However—" He broke off when a maid came skidding into the room.

"Where is Mr. Baldwin?" the girl cried.

"He just left with the deliveryman," Mrs. McPhee said. "What is wrong, Dora?"

The girl cast a nervous glance Valan's way. He raised a brow. "M-Mr. Baldwin will w-want to see what is going on in the ballroom," she stammered.

"Dare I ask what is going on in the ballroom?" Valan asked.

"They are bringing in chairs and tables for the party, but a leg has broken off one chair, an arm off another, and a table is sitting crooked," the girl answered.

"I am surrounded by people who intend to destroy all I own," Valan muttered.

The maid nodded vigorously. "I think you're right, my lord. But that is no' all."

"God help me," he said.

"They're bringing in candles. Too many, I think."

"A broken table or chair I will forgive, but I cannot allow my house to be burnt down," he said. "I am startled to realize how incompetent is my staff."

"We are not incompetent," Mrs. McPhee said. "I saved you from being bilked by that deliveryman. As for the chairs and tables, they are old."

"Old?" Valan repeated. "I had no idea I owned 'old' furniture."

"Ye havenae had a party in fifteen years," the housekeeper said. "We don't keep all those chairs and tables out. They are being brought down from the attic. Those in the ballroom, well, some of them are probably rotted."

"Has it really been fifteen years since you've thrown a party?" Jeanine asked.

He nodded slowly. "So it would seem."

Footsteps sounded in the hallway. An instant later, Baldwin entered. "The deliveryman has departed," he announced.

"Is there a reason for this announcement?" Valan asked.

"There is another delivery," Baldwin replied.

"I'll see to it." Mrs. McPhee started to turn.

"Mrs. McPhee," Valan said, "I beg you, do not beat this deliveryman. I would rather not have goods shipped in from England because all of Edinburgh's merchants are afraid of my housekeeper. Baldwin, please have my carriage brought round. I must fetch help before it is too late."

CHAPTER 6

VALAN ARRIVED WITH MISS MATHESON AND MISS STONE AT HIS cousin's home and directed the servant to escort the ladies to the garden. He then went to the drawing room where he was told his cousin rested. Legs curled up beneath her skirts on a pale yellow divan, Peigi rested her chin on her arm, which was stretched out across the divan back. She turned her gaze from the window overlooking the east lawn.

"Valan, what a surprise." She straightened and extended a hand.

He dutifully crossed the room, grasped her fingers and bowed over them. "You are looking well," he said.

She sighed. "Well, I am not well."

Valan sat on the far end of the divan. "Are you ill?"

"Don't be ridiculous. You know I am never sick. Nae, it is Richard. He is intolerable."

"Ah, what has your husband done now?" Valan asked.

She pouted. "You needn't act as if it is he who must tolerate me. I know how you men are."

"Indeed?"

"Yes, you protect one another."

"If that is true, it is only because women are such formidable foes."

"There you are," she cried. "Why must men see women as foes?"

"I doubt I could explain it to your satisfaction," he said.

"Because the notion is ridiculous," she replied.

"You are probably right. In any case, I did not come here to discuss the male mind. I need your help."

"My help?" Her brows rose. "I have never known you to ask anyone for help."

"Be that as it may, I am doing so now. I am planning a party and would like you to help."

"A party?" She frowned. "You never throw parties."

"I admit, it has been some time."

She regarded him. "What are you up to?"

"I am not 'up to' anything. I have simply taken a ward and am introducing her into society."

"Her?" Peigi stiffened. "You are mistaken, sir, if you think I will be party to your *affaire de coeur*."

"This is no affair," he replied mildly.

"No one will be fooled by the pretense—least of all Richard. You know he will never allow me to associate with one of your light o' loves. Besides, I know you too well."

"Pray tell, what do you know?"

"I know that you do not do anything that doesn't benefit you. Don't be cross," she quickly added. "We all have our faults and that is yours. I love you, nonetheless."

"I am grateful. However, despite your…accurate assessment of my character, Miss Matheson is, indeed, my ward and nothing more."

"I don't believe you."

"My dear, Peigi, have you ever noted amongst my, er, short-comings, that I am a liar?"

Her brow furrowed. "Well, not exactly."

He lifted a brow.

She rolled her eyes. "Oh, all right. But it's not because you aren't capable of it."

He laughed. "If you are to condemn me for what I can do, instead of what I have done, you might as well sentence me to the gallows this instant."

She shuddered. "Nothing so dramatic."

He angled his head. "Thank you. Now, I expect you to accord Miss Matheson all the respect due my ward."

She narrowed her eyes. "I warn you, Valan, I will not be made a fool. If I discover she is not who you say she is—"

"Your warnings are unwarranted, my dear. You may recall that I am quite strict when it comes to your reputation."

"Well." Peigi smoothed her skirt. "That is true." She giggled. "Remember when you challenged poor Mr. Nicholson to a duel? I vow, I was sure you would kill him and be forced to flee to France—or worse, the Colonies."

"I believe it is you who is now being dramatic," he said.

"Not at all. That really was quite foolish of you. All over a kiss."

"While I am not known for bending the truth, you are. We both know it was more than a kiss."

Her eyes flashed. "Not so much to be worth a duel."

"Make no mistake, that is due only to the fact that I challenged him."

"You act as if I don't have a brain," she said.

He gave a low laugh. "You do, indeed, have a brain. That is what makes you so dangerous."

She narrowed her eyes. "I see. Women are your foes because we have a brain."

"If it were only your brains, we would be in no danger," he said with another laugh.

She lifted her chin. "You cannot blame us for being beautiful."

"Indeed, we can. But forget this silly debate. Come, I wish to show you my ward."

"You brought her here?" Peigi demanded.

"Of course." He sighed when her eyes narrowed. "Remember, Peigi, I will not compromise you. Please, have a look and you will see for yourself that she is nothing more than a child." He rose and extended a hand toward her.

"I can never really be angry with you." She laid a delicate hand in his and allowed him to pull her to her feet.

He led her from the drawing room and into a small study that overlooked the garden. To the far left, Miss Stone sat on the granite bench beside the rose bushes.

"Valan, she is twenty-five years old, if she's a day—and she is so demure. I can well believe you are not dallying with her but—" She broke off when Miss Matheson came into view. "What—" She looked up at him. "Her?"

He nodded. "Her."

Peigi returned her attention to the window. "She's quite beautiful. You can't expect me to believe—"

"I expect you to believe exactly what I've told you," he cut in.

She cast him a startled glance, then watched Miss Matheson for another moment before turning away from the window. "Why do you need my help with the party? You have servants."

"All fools," he said. "They will destroy every piece of furniture I own, then burn the house down in a funerary pyre."

"Lord, Valan, you're in a mood. What is wrong?"

"I would like this ball to go off well," he replied.

She studied him. "You are serious."

"I am," he replied. Still, she hesitated. Valan crossed to the bell pull near the door and rang for a servant.

"What are you doing?" Peigi asked.

"Introducing you to Miss Matheson."

A young maid appeared a moment later and Valan bade her

bring Miss Matheson and Miss Stone to the sitting room. He returned with his cousin to the room and, a moment later, the maid brought the two women.

Jeanine's eyes met his and her face lit with a smile. "Did you see the roses, Grey? They are the most beautiful I have ever seen."

"We are not at home, Jeanine," he said. "You will address me as 'sir' or 'my lord.'"

"But this is your cousin's home. She is family." Her eyes shifted to Peigi. "Is this her? Of course, you are her," she went on before anyone could reply. Jeanine hurried across the room to the couch where Peigi sat. She gave a pretty curtsey then clapped her hands. "You are beautiful. Of course, I knew you would be. I wish I had blonde hair like yours. Mine is plain old brown. Your blue dress compliments your hair perfectly. Do you like Miss Stone's dress? Oh dear, we haven't introduced you to Miss Stone. How rude." Jeanine looked at Valan

"I was waiting for you to finish, my dear."

She wrinkled her nose. "Is that your way of saying that I talk too much?" She grinned. "You may proceed, *sir*."

He angled his head in thanks, then said, "Peigi, as you must have guessed, this is my ward Miss Jeanine Matheson, and this is her companion, Miss Stone."

Miss Stone curtsied and murmured, "My lady."

"Do you like Miss Stone's dress?" Jeanine asked. "Mrs. Morgan made it for her. I did her hair, but I think you could do better."

Peigi blinked. "I beg your pardon?"

"Your hair is so beautifully done that I know you can help Miss Stone with hers. I am only tolerably good at styling a lady's hair."

"Of course, I know how to style a lady's hair," Peigi said, "But it is Matilda who styled mine."

"But you directed her, I'm sure," Jeanine said. "And you would accept nothing less than perfection."

"That is true," Peigi demurred.

Jeanine beamed. "Would you do her hair for the party? You are coming, of course?"

Peigi looked at Valan and he lifted a brow. "Well, my dear," he said, "will you be attending?"

CHAPTER 7

THE NEXT TEN DAYS FLEW BY AND JEANINE WAS SURPRISED TO find that the marquess was right. In his large home, she saw him but half a dozen times, and then only in passing. He had promised to attend tonight's party, but still, it was only just after breakfast, and waiting until the evening seemed an interminable amount of time not to see him. He made no appearance and Miss Stone's efforts to divert her attention were for naught.

"Perhaps we could shop for a fan to match the ivory gown you're to wear." Miss Stone finished refilling their teacups, then returned the pot to the tray and lifted her cup from the coffee table. "Mrs. Morgan suggested a fan."

Jeanine clasped the top edge of the sofa back and rested her cheek against her hand. "Do you think Grey doesn't like me anymore?"

"Of course, he likes you," Miss Stone said. "What would make you think otherwise?" She met Jeanine's gaze and sipped her tea.

"He's never around," Jeanine replied.

"He is an important man. I'm sure that business keeps him busy."

Jeanine sighed. "But it's almost as if he's avoiding me."

"I haven't noticed anything like that," Miss Stone said.

"Really? You're not trying to spare my feelings?"

"No, ma'am. I would never think of being anything less than honest with you."

Jeanine beamed. "That's what I like best about you, Miss Stone. You're not like so many others who only say what benefits them."

Miss Stone smiled serenely. "I have never been a good liar."

Jeanine laughed. "You say that as if it is a bad thing."

"There are times when it is best not to be forthcoming."

Jeanine grimaced. "You're right, of course. I often get into trouble by being too honest."

"Are you sure you don't want to go shopping? You will want to please his lordship by looking your best."

Jeanine lifted her head. "You're right."

Forty-five minutes later, they entered a small shop that sold only the finest ladies' fans. Jeanine took no more than ten minutes to choose a plain bone fan with a single hummingbird painted on it.

They left the shop and Jeanine linked arms with Miss Stone. "We are off on a special errand, Miss Stone."

Miss Stone looked at Jeanine, her expression perfect politeness, and she said, "Indeed, Miss Matheson?"

Jeanine nodded. "Indeed."

They waited for two passing couples, then started across the walk to their carriage. Their footman, seated next to Mr. Potts, the driver, spotted them and stood from the driver's seat. He leapt down and opened the coach door.

Jeanine brought herself and Miss Stone to a stop and shook her head. "We will be walking." She looked up at the driver.

"Mr. Potts, can you tell me where we can find a shop that sells cravats?"

"I beg your pardon, Miss, cravats?"

She nodded.

"You want to go to a men's shop, Miss?"

"That is where they sell cravats," she said.

"Are you sure, Miss?"

"Sure that is where they sell men's cravats?" she asked. "Of course. Where else would I buy a cravat?"

"No, Miss. I mean, are you sure you want to go there? Ladies do not generally shop at a gentleman's clothing store," he said.

"How silly," she said. "If you do not know where a shop is, I'm sure I can get the direction from a passerby."

"Nae," he hurriedly replied. "In fact, I know the shop where his lordship gets his cravats."

"Perfect,' Jeanine cried. "Where is it?"

He exchanged a look with the footman, who shrugged, then said, "It isn't far. I will take you and Miss Stone."

"It's too beautiful a day to ride. We will walk. Just direct us, please."

His eyes widened in horror. "I cannae let you walk alone."

"Don't be silly," she said. "Where is the shop?"

He shook his head stubbornly. "His lordship will dismiss me if I let you walk alone—after he beat me, that is."

"Mr. Potts is right," Miss Stone said. "If you are set on walking, our footman should accompany us."

Jeanine smiled. "How clever of you."

The driver finally gave them directions, but said he would follow with the carriage so that he could take them home from the shop. They reached the shop in ten minutes and entered. To the left, two brown leather chairs resided near the window, separated by a table that held a tray containing a decanter of amber liquid and four glasses. To the right, shelves displayed cravats, hats, and other sundry man's articles in a multitude of colors.

A tall, wiry man, writing in a ledger, stood behind the long counter at the far end of the shop. He looked up and frowned. "May I help you?"

Jeanine crossed to the counter with Miss Stone alongside, and said, "We are looking for a cravat."

His frown deepened. "Are you sure you're in the right shop?"

"You do sell cravats," Jeanine said. "I see lots there on the shelves."

The man stiffened. "We sell *gentlemen's* cravats."

"I beg your pardon?" Miss Stone said. "A *gentleman's* cravat is exactly what Miss Matheson is looking for. She is shopping for the Marquess of Northington."

The man's eyes narrowed. "His lordship does buy his cravats here. But I feel certain you have the wrong shop. Ladies who purchase cravats—"

"This lady is Lord Northington's ward," Miss Stone cut in.

The man blinked in surprise, then his mouth thinned. "His lordship sends me an order when he desires more cravats. He does not send his *ward* to purchase them for him."

"You misunderstand," Jeanine said. "Gre-er, his lordship did not send me. I am buying him a gift."

"I believe I understand perfectly well, Miss."

"I am certain you do not," Miss Stone said in a chilly voice that startled Jeanine. "His lordship will not be pleased to hear that the man who sells him his cravats was so shockingly rude to his ward." She looked down her nose at him and waited.

Fifteen minutes later, they left the shop with a lovely ivory cravat, along with a dusky blue cravat, purchased at Miss Stone's suggestion. She said the color would complement Grey's dark eyes, and Jeanine was certain she was right. Their carriage sat in front of the shop with Mr. Potts in the driver seat and the footman waiting at the door. He opened the door as they approached, but Jeanine slowed at sight of another shop across the street. A sign over the door read Branby's Furniture and in the window were displayed chairs and tables.

"There's a shop across the street I would like to look at," Jeanine said, and started toward the street.

"Miss," Mr. Potts cried, "I must object. His lordship would not want you going about the city unescorted."

"Then we are in no danger of upsetting him." She waved a dismissive hand. "Miss Stone accompanies me, and you and Mr. McKinnon are only a few steps away."

Mr. Potts leapt from his perch and hurried to the curb as Jeanine and Miss Stone crossed the street. They reached the shop and entered. The room was nicely furnished with two chairs, a couch, two tables with lamps, and a sideboard that bore a crystal decanter and half a dozen tumblers.

A stalky man emerged from a curtained door behind a counter in the far left-hand corner of the room and halted. "May I help you?"

"I was hoping to purchase a table for Lord Northington," Jeanine said

The man frowned. "The Marquess of Northington?"

She nodded. "But it seems you don't have what I want."

The shopkeeper drew himself up. "My shop carries only the highest quality furniture. Perhaps something on Glenmore Street would be more to your taste."

"Miss Matheson is the Marquess of Northington's ward," Miss Stone said. "She does not shop on Glenmore Street."

The man frowned. "I hadn't heard he took a ward."

"He has," Miss Stone said in a chilly voice. "In fact, he's throwing a ball in her honor this very evening."

The man's head snapped in Jeanine's direction.

She nodded enthusiastically. "Perhaps you would like to come."

His eyes widened.

"I'm not certain his lordship would be pleased," Miss Stone said.

"He said I could invite guests," Jeanine said.

"He said you could invite friends from Lady Paddington's School for Young Ladies," Miss Stone pointed out.

Jeanine waved a dismissive hand. "Oh, pooh. It makes no difference." She smiled at the shopkeeper. "Surely, you would like to come? You know where we live, of course."

The man remained mute, but shook his head.

"Never mind," she said. "I can write it down for you. Oh, it is a shame you don't have a game table. You see, he had a game table, but it was broken, and it is my fault because Mrs. McPhee and the deliveryman got into a row."

"A row?" the man repeated.

She nodded. "Mrs. McPhee was angry with the deliveryman because she was certain he was trying to cheat Grey. I like Mrs. McPhee, but I think it was just a mistake. The deliveryman delivered too many vegetables--according to Mrs. McPhee, you understand. Gr-er, his lordship said he didn't think they were enough vegetables. They had a terrible disagreement and Mrs. McPhee punched him in the jaw."

"Punched him in the jaw?" the man mimicked.

"Exactly," Jeanine said. "Mrs. McPhee uses her right hand to knead dough, which means she is very strong. I think that is very fortunate, for a woman must be able to defend herself. Don't you agree?" She smiled before he could answer, and added, "Of course you do. When Mrs. McPhee punched the deliveryman, he crashed into the marquess's game table. So, if not for the fact that he was throwing this party in my honor, the deliveryman would never have come, and he and Mrs. McPhee would never have been fighting, and the table wouldn't have been broken. That makes it my fault. He didn't complain—the marquess, I mean—but he wouldn't, for his manners are too good." She slanted a glance at Miss Stone. "Isn't that so, Miss Stone?"

"Indeed, it is," she replied.

"There you are," Jeanine said. "The table was a very nice table, so it is only fair I should replace it." She sighed. "I do wish you had one."

The shopkeeper blinked. "But I do have one."

"You do?" she exclaimed. "Why didn't you say so in the first place?"

The man looked helplessly at Miss Stone, who shrugged. He sighed in obvious resignation and said, "If you will follow me, please," then turned.

He led them through the curtained door into a large storeroom crammed full of furniture. They weaved through the cramped rows and she spotted the game table beside a hideous green divan. When they reached the table, Jeanine knew it was exactly what she'd been looking for. The black and white checkered marble top was flawless. The dark wood, cherrywood, she guessed, perfectly complemented the marble. A drawer on the left side might hold cards and chess pieces while a lower shelf provided extra storage.

"It's beautiful," she breathed. "Do you like it, Miss Stone?"

"I believe his lordship will be very pleased," she said.

Jeanine looked at the shopkeeper. "Can you deliver it today, please?"

"Today? I would have to get a deliveryman."

Jeanine laughed. "Just be careful to bring only the table, or Mrs. McPhee is liable to punch him." The man's eyes widened, and Jeanine added, "No need to worry. I'll make sure she understands the table is to be delivered. Please say you can do it today. It would be a great favor, as the ball is this evening and I so want to surprise him beforehand. I must give you the address. That way you will know where to come to the party tonight."

"I am certain the Marquess of Northington would not include me on his guest list," the shopkeeper said.

"Why not? The party begins at eight. No one arrives at eight, I think—if they want to be fashionable, that is. But, of course, you know that." She smiled again and wondered why the shopkeeper had gone pale.

CHAPTER 8

"You are so clever to suggest a walk in the park." Jeanine turned her face to the sun and slowed her walk alongside Lady Guilford. She closed her eyes and concentrated on the soft warmth that seemed to penetrate her bones. "I believe I was driving poor Miss Stone to distraction looking for something to do. She must be glad for a little time away from me."

"Walking is very good for the constitution," Lady Guilford said.

Jeanine opened her eyes in time to avoid a large bump in the path. "My mother often walks the path from our house to town," she said.

"Where is your town?" Lady Guilford asked.

"Perth."

A young couple passed them. Lady Guilford acknowledged them with a graceful cant of her head and they responded in kind. "Your mother allowed you to come to Edinburgh alone?" she asked when they'd passed the man and woman.

Jeanine shook her head. "Joshua brought me—well, he and my youngest sister and her husband. I suppose that means

Rebecca and her husband are who brought me. Though it was Joshua's wagon and he drove."

"Who, pray tell, is Joshua?" asked Lady Guilford.

Jeanine spotted a butterfly hovering over a patch of lush heather, just off the path. "A lad I grew up with," she said as they approached, and the butterfly flitted away.

Lady Guilford cast her a sideways glance. "It was kind of this childhood friend to bring you all the way to Edinburgh."

"He is kind that way."

"I see. Will he take you back home?"

Jeanine looked sharply at her. "I don't plan to return. Grey promised to help me find an elderly husband."

Lady Guilford raised brow. "An elderly husband?"

Jeanine nodded. "Aye. I plan to use his money to open a school like Lady Peddington's."

Behind them, a creak of wheels approached and a phaeton passed them on a coach path to their left.

"I suppose Joshua doesn't approve of the idea of you running a ladies' school," Lady Guilford said.

Jeanine made a face. "Not in the least. He believes ladies should stay at home to cook, clean, and have their husband's children."

"He could not have been happy you preferred Edinburgh to marrying him."

"He wasn't at all pleased." Jeanine caught herself and frowned. "You tricked me. That was unkind of you."

"Not at all," Lady Guilford replied. "Is there some reason you would want to keep secret the fact that you have an admirer?"

"Nae," Jeanine hedged.

Lady Guilford gave her a penetrating stare and waited.

Jeanine relaxed. "It's just that if I don't find a gentleman to marry then I will have to return home and marry Joshua. I would be stuck in his cottage all day with a dozen of his children."

"Perhaps not a dozen," Lady Guilford said with a half-smile.

"One is too many," Jeanine said.

Lady Guilford sidestepped a rock. "Do you not want children?"

"They are a great deal of trouble," Jeanine said. "Do you have children?"

"Nae."

"There you go. You understand."

Lady Guilford nodded, but something in the slight down-turn of her mouth gave Jeanine pause.

"Surely, there are men to choose from other than Joshua," Lady Guilford said. "You are young. Go home and let the young men court you."

Jeanine shook her head. "Oh, I can never return home," Jeanine replied. "My mother has remarried."

"Your mother has remarried," Lady Guilford began, then broke off when a man turned onto the path up ahead.

He neared. Something about him seemed familiar. Lady Guilford whispered unintelligible words under her breath. In the next instant, Jeanine recognized Lord Gordon. He lifted a hand and waved, then called out to them as he quickened his step.

He reached them, and they were forced to stop when he halted and bowed. "Lady Guilford, what a pleasure to see you."

"Lord Gordon," she replied in a cool voice.

He seemed not to notice, and looked at Jeanine. "A pleasure to see you, Miss Matheson. I did not know you liked to walk."

Jeanine followed Lady Guilford's example and replied in an aloof tone, "Of course, everyone likes to walk."

He smiled. "Quite right. May I have the pleasure of your company for the remainder of your stroll?" The question seemed directed at Jeanine, which struck her as rude, for he should have addressed Lady Guilford.

"We will be returning home soon," Lady Guilford said.

"It would be a pleasure to accompany you however far you go," he said, clearly oblivious to her reticence.

To Jeanine's surprise, he stepped to her right and winged an arm toward her. Jeanine looked at Lady Guilford for approval. She gave a curt nod and Jeanine wondered if she'd done something wrong, but slipped her hand into the crook of his arm.

"How is Lord Guilford, my lady?" he asked, and covered Jeanine's hand with his as they started forward.

"Quite well, thank you," she said.

Jeanine resisted the urge to pull her hand free of his as he prattled on about the weather, how lovely they both looked, and confirmed that they remained in good health.

"You must be terribly busy with plans for the ball your cousin is hosting tonight, Lady Guilford."

She gave a careless laugh. "No more than usual."

"I do believe all of Edinburgh is talking about the party," he said.

"It will likely be the ball of the season," she replied casually.

"With you at the helm, success is assured," he said. "Miss Matheson, you must be looking forward to this evening."

"Oh yes. I don't think I have ever attended a ball quite so large. Grey says at least three hundred people should attend. I'm not sure his ballroom will hold that many."

Lady Guilford shot her a warning look, and said, "Of course, it will."

A carriage rattled past followed by two men on horseback.

"It is certainly larger than any ball I have attended," Lord Gordon said.

"I cannot believe Gre—"

Lady Guilford looked sharply at her.

Jeanine realized her mistake, and amended, "—his lordship knows so many people."

"He is the Marquess of Northington and 6th Earl of Edmonds," Lord Gordon said. "He knows everyone."

"He is an earl, as well as a marquess?" Jeanine laughed. "I didn't know that."

They came to a Y in the path. Left, led to town. To the right, their carriage waited at the edge of the trees up ahead. They angled right. As they approached the carriage, the driver opened the door and stood aside.

Lord Gordon helped Lady Guilford into the carriage, then Jeanine. He grasped the door, then hesitated and said, "Forgive me for being forward, Miss Matheson, but I hope that I might call on you sometime soon at Finley Hall."

Jeanine started.

"You would have to speak with Valan about that," Lady Guilford interjected. "The ball is tonight, so he is busy, of course, and I believe he has business through next week."

His face fell, and he said in such a forlorn voice, "Of course," that Jeanine said, "We will see you at the ball?"

Hope lit his expression, and she was relieved when he looked to Lady Guilford for confirmation.

"Of course, you are coming," she said, but her words lacked warmth.

He beamed. "Most kind of you. I wouldn't think of missing it. Until tonight."

He closed the door and Lady Guilford stared out the window as the carriage rolled past the trees. They reached the street and the silence closed in on Jeanine.

"I have done something wrong, haven't I?" she said.

Lady Guilford looked at her. "I beg your pardon?"

"I know that I forget to call Grey 'his lordship' when we are in public. He told me I must do so, but his name is out of my mouth before I realize it. I am sorry. I know it's very improper."

"You must try to remember. Valan does not want any scandal associated with you."

"Why would there be scandal associated with me?"

Lady Guilford hesitated. "There won't be, so long as you conduct yourself appropriately."

Jeanine regarded her. "You don't like Lord Gordon very much. I don't think Grey likes him, either. I must admit, he can be annoying."

"He is much more than annoying," Lady Guilford said under her breath.

"Why do you think he asked to call on me?" Jeanine asked.

Lady Guilford snorted. "Because he cannot countenance Valan having something he does not."

Jeanine frowned. "You mean me."

Startlement crossed Lady Guilford's face. "Put my words out of your mind. I am talking out of place. Something Valan will not quickly forgive."

"I don't have to tell him that you said that. Not that is matters," Jeanine added. "I have no idea what you mean."

"Then there is no harm done," she replied. "Let's not mention it again."

"If you say so," Jeanine said, but she couldn't help thinking harm had been done.

Valan entered his house and paused in the foyer. The bustle of party preparations filtered throughout the mansion. The indistinct murmur of voices, the distant rattle of pots, quick footsteps. Clearly, the majority of the work had been done. Things were quiet compared to the tension and harried air that had permeated the house until yesterday.

He strode down the hallway to his library and went inside, pulling the door closed behind him. The faint noise cut off, and quiet descended. He hadn't been certain he would survive the preparations, but he had. He started for the sideboard located against the wall to the right of the hearth, then halted at sight of the game table sitting where his old game table had been.

He didn't remember buying a new table. Valan crossed to the table and stared at it. He traced a finger across the exquisite inlaid marble. The table might very well be finer than the one he had owned—even if it hadn't been in his family for three generations.

He slid open the drawer on the left-hand side and found inside the cards and game pieces that had filled the other table's drawer. Baldwin must've taken the liberty of replacing the table, which surprised him. Baldwin knew Valan's taste as well as he did himself, and the steward had not failed on this point, but Valan had never known him to take such initiative. Still, he couldn't complain.

A knock sounded on the door and Baldwin entered. "Forgive the interruption, sir, but you have a visitor. Baron Rosemund."

"Show him in," Valan said. Baldwin started to turn, and Valan said, "Baldwin, I must thank you for the game table."

The steward shook his head. "I did not procure the table for you, sir. I believe that was Miss Matheson's doing."

"Indeed?" Valan replied. "Wonders never cease."

Baldwin left, and a moment later reappeared with Brendan. Baldwin bowed and closed the door as he left.

"I believe Baldwin grows more dour by the year," the baron said. "How long have you employed him?"

"Fifteen years," Valan said.

"Perhaps that explains his somber mood."

Valan gave him a dry look, then headed for the sideboard. "Have you come here simply to abuse me?"

Brendan laughed. "Forgive me. But you must admit that I am right."

Valan poured two glasses of sherry. "I must admit nothing of the sort. The party is tonight, my dear. You're very early and not dressed for the evening. Don't tell me you're here to say you cannot attend. I have plans for you tonight."

He crossed to his desk, handed Brendan one of the glasses, then motioned to the chairs that faced the low-burning fire in the hearth.

"The knowledge you have plans for me is enough to have me come down with a fever and cry off," the baron said as he settled into one of the chairs. "What are these plans?"

"What would be the fun if I told you?" Valan replied.

"None for you, I imagine. I'm here to ask if you heard that Latham left Edinburgh."

Valan sipped his sherry. "I believe I did hear that bit of gossip."

"I fear it is more than gossip, Valan. He is nowhere to be found."

"One need only know where to look," Valan said.

Brandan's eyes narrowed. "You know where he is."

"I not only know where he is, I sent him there."

Brendan released a breath. "Then we need not worry on account of our investment."

"You need not," Valan said. "Though Latham will no longer be handling our business."

"What? But you said— What have you done?" Brendan asked.

"It is best you not ask," Valan answered. "Just rest easy that our investments are now in the hands of someone who won't try to steal them."

Shock registered on Brendan's face. "Embezzlement?"

"Attempted embezzlement," Valan said.

"Who's in charge now?" the baron asked.

Valan took another sip of sherry and smiled.

"Never say you are handling the shipments?" Brendan said. "Good God."

"Should I take offense?" Valan asked.

"What?" Brendan gave a distracted shake of his head. "Nae, it's just a shock. Embezzlement, and you running the company."

"Just long enough for us to receive payment," Valan said.

"Everyone will be glad to hear you took charge and saved us."

"Let us not say anything just yet," Valan said.

Brendan regarded him. "Johnston may not be too pleased."

"Nor Anthony."

Brendan nodded. "I will leave everything to you."

"Very sensible. Now, do you—"

Voices sounded outside the door and a quick knock followed, then the door opened and Jeanine and Miss Stone entered.

Jeanine clutched a flat box. When her gaze met Valan's, her face brightened. "I told you he was here." She hurried toward him. Miss Stone followed at a sedate pace.

"My God," Brendan murmured.

The ladies reached them and Valan and Brendan rose. Jeanine curtsied and looked up at Brendan. "Hello, sir."

"Brendan, this is my ward, Miss Matheson," Valan said. "Jeanine, may I present Baron Rosemund."

Brendan bowed over her hand. "A pleasure, Miss Matheson."

"How do you do, sir?" Jeanine replied, and before Valan could introduce Miss Stone, Jeanine said, "This is my friend, Miss Stone."

Brendan bowed over her hand. "Ma'am. Please, have my seat," he told Jeanine. I will fetch a chair for Miss Stone and myself."

"How very kind of you," Jeanine said. "Miss Stone, you sit. I have sat enough for today." Miss Stone took the offered chair and Jeanine then turned to Valan. "Did you see the table? Is it not beautiful? We found it today when we were shopping for this." She extended the box.

He took it. "What is this?"

She smiled. "Open it and find out, silly."

Brendan didn't successfully stifle his laughter. Valan removed the top and started at sight of two exquisite cravats lying side by side: one ivory, the other a dark blue.

He looked at Jeanine. "What are these for?"

"They're cravats. They're to wear," she said.

More low laughter from Brendan, who had placed another chair beside Miss Stone's chair.

"So, I see," Valan said. "To what do I owe the honor of this gift?"

"My mother says a man can never have too many cravats. I intended only to purchase the ivory, but Miss Stone said the blue would complement your eyes." Jeanine lifted the blue cravat and held it against his temple. She smiled. "She was right —not that I doubted her." Jeanine laid the cravat back in the box. "Do you not like them? Was my mother wrong, do you have too many cravats?"

"Never," he said. "The blue is particularly nice, and I don't believe I have one that color. Thank you."

"Shall we sit?" He pointed to his chair.

She shook her head. "We only came to give you the cravats and to see if you like the table. Do you like the table? You didn't say so. Oh dear, did we miscalculate? I was so sure you would like it."

"If you will permit me to explain," he said, "it is exquisite."

She beamed. "I knew you would like it. Well, we must go. Lady Guilford was very specific in saying that we must begin preparation for the party no later than six." Jeanine leaned close to him and said in a conspiratorial whisper, "She is a little frightening."

He laughed. "Indeed, she is."

"I plan to cheat just a little and go to the kitchen first and beg some chocolate and pastries from Mrs. McPhee," Jeanine said. "But we must be certain there is no chocolate left on our mouths when Lady Guilford arrives."

"Heaven forbid," he agreed with all seriousness.

"If you are ready, Miss Stone," Jeanine said.

Miss Stone stood. She nodded to Valan and Brendan, and murmured, "My lords," then started toward the door alongside Jeanine.

Jeanine halted and looked over her shoulder at Valan. "You will be at the ball?"

"Of course."

She nodded, and they left.

Valan reclaimed his seat beside Brendan.

"I don't believe it," Brendan said.

"Believe what, my dear?"

"She is not at all what I expected."

Valan looked at him. "What did you expect?"

"Well…a femme fatale, I suppose."

"Goodness, why would you expect that?"

Branden lifted a brow and grinned. "Because, my friend, that is the only kind of woman I've ever seen you with."

"Ah, I see your error." Valan finished off his sherry. "I am not 'with' Miss Matheson."

Brendan laughed. "Does she know that?"

CHAPTER 9

JEANINE SCANNED THE CROWDED BALLROOM. "I DON'T SEE GREY anywhere. Do you, Miss Stone? Your superior height gives you an advantage."

"I am afraid I don't. It would seem everyone who received an invitation is here. I have never seen such a crowded ballroom."

"Oh, I see him," Jeanine said. "Is that him in the far left corner talking to that redheaded woman?"

"I believe you're right," Miss Stone said.

"We better hurry before we lose him," Jeanine said, and started forward.

Miss Stone kept up with her, oftentimes parting the way when people didn't see Jeanine.

"You're so fortunate to be tall," Jeanine said.

"If you say so, Miss Matheson."

They skirted a large crowd of women and Jeanine spotted the marquess with the woman.

"She's standing too close to him. Don't you agree, Miss Stone?" Jeanine said in a whisper.

"The ladies today are too fast," Miss Stone said in a prim voice.

The woman leaned even closer to him and laughed at something he said. Jeanine and Miss Stone neared him and he looked past the woman at Jeanine. She came to a stop in front of him with Miss Stone beside her.

His lordship smiled. "Good evening, Miss Matheson."

"Good evening, *sir*," she said.

Amusement tugged at his mouth. "Lady Claire, may I introduce my ward, Miss Matheson. Jeanine, this is Lady Claire."

Jeanine curtsied. "My lady."

Lady Claire gave a slight nod.

"And this is her companion, Miss Stone," the marquess said. "Miss Stone, I present Lady Claire."

Miss Stone curtsied. "My lady."

Lady Claire angled her head in a graceful nod.

"Are you enjoying the party?" he asked Jeanine.

She nodded. "It's very exciting. Miss Stone has already danced with two gentlemen."

The marquess smiled politely. "How very fortunate for the gentlemen."

"Lady Guilford made introductions," Miss Stone said. "The gentlemen could do no less than ask me to dance."

"That is not so." Jeanine looked at the marquess. "I am correct, am I not?"

"Quite correct," he agreed. "Rest assured, Miss Stone, my cousin simply knows how to pair up good dancers."

Miss Stone angled her head in acquiescence. "As you say, my lord."

Jeanine caught sight of a tall, wiry man standing just beyond the dance floor, scanning the large ballroom. "How grand. Look, Miss Stone, it is Mr. Craig." She nodded in his direction.

"Mr. Craig?" the marquess asked.

"I must fetch him," Jeanine said.

"Allow me," Miss Stone said, and started away.

"May I ask, who is Mr. Craig?" his lordship asked.

"Of course. You will not be surprised," Jeanine said.

"I pray not, but I am curious to know how you made the acquaintance of a gentleman I am unaware of."

Jeanine laughed. "You're not unaware of him—not really. He is the gentleman who owns the shop where I purchased the game table."

"Game table?' Lady Claire repeated.

"Aye," Jeanine said. "I had to replace it because—"

"I think we can forego the telling of that tedious story," Grey interrupted.

Jeanine's heart fell. "Aye."

Miss Stone arrived with Mr. Craig. She made introductions and Mr. Craig bowed stiffly. "My lord, I hope I am not intruding. Miss Matheson was quite adamant that I attend. If this is an intrusion, I understand."

"Not in the least," the marquess said. "Miss Matheson may invite anyone she likes. You are welcome at Finley Hall."

Jeanine caught the look of surprise that Lady Claire couldn't quite hide.

The marquess introduced Mr. Craig to Lady Claire. The man bowed low again and Jeanine wondered if he might break in half.

The orchestra struck up a waltz. "A waltz," she cried. "How enlightened of you to have the orchestra play a waltz, sir. This is perfect. You promised me a dance."

His lordship lifted a brow. "I don't remember that promise."

"Oh yes, you did—and you cannot say you have forgotten because you are old, because you are not."

"But if I have forgotten, then it must be from age."

She grinned. "Then you admit you promised."

"Very clever, my dear, but I admit nothing of the kind."

She shrugged. "I suppose if you cannot remember, I will have to settle for dancing with Lord Pomeroy."

"Lord Pomeroy is not the sort of man you should dance with, particularly the waltz."

"But I promised. I cannot break my promise."

His eyes narrowed slightly, then he addressed Lady Claire. "You'll have to excuse me, Lady Claire."

She gave him a pretty pout, and Jeanine repressed a roll of her eyes when the pout leaked into her voice, "But you promised me a walk, my lord." She looked at him through her lashes. "I feel certain you have not forgotten *that* promise."

He caught her hand and brushed his lips across her fingers. "I have not forgotten. But that will have to wait." He released her hand, and turned. "Sir," he said to Mr. Craig, and then to Miss Stone, "Miss Stone."

Jeanine glimpsed the startlement on Lady Claire's face before the woman's eyes narrowed. Then his lordship cupped Jeanine's elbow and turned her toward the dance floor.

At the edge of the dance floor, he swung her into his arms, his right hand pressed lightly against her back, his left clasping her right hand. He stepped back to arm's length, then pulled her into the music with flawless rhythm. He steered them around a couple who nearly collided with them, then turned her in a tight circle that took her breath. Jeanine laughed, and when she looked up at him, he was smiling down at her. She smiled back and slid right as the press of his hand on her back cued her.

"You are an excellent dancer," she said. "Not at all too old."

"I never said I couldn't dance." His express turned serious. "I would prefer you didn't dance with Lord Pomeroy."

"Is he a rake?" she asked.

"He is."

"You are afraid my reputation will be tarnished."

"Something like that," he said.

She shrugged. "I don't really like him."

"But you would have danced with him, despite my request that you not."

"I will not dance with him, if you prefer I don't."

"That's very generous of you, considering you coerced me into dancing with you."

She gave him a bright smile.

An answering smile tugged at the corners of his mouth before he said in mock sternness, "Perhaps it isn't you I need worry about, but the gentlemen you bewitch."

She laughed again and said no more.

Three dances later, Mr. Westland escorted Jeanine from the dance floor and she had to admit she was fatigued.

"You look as though you could use some refreshment," he said.

They approached a large alcove, but Jeanine stopped when it seemed he might continue inside. Lady Guilford had been very specific in her instructions that Jeanine was, under no condition, to enter an alcove alone with any gentleman.

She looked up at Mr. Westland. "I am thirsty."

He smiled. "Let me fetch you some punch."

She gave him a grateful smile before he left. Jeanine looked for a place to sit, but there was no place, save the alcove. She considered. After all, she wasn't with a gentleman, so she wouldn't be disobeying Lady Guilford. Jeanine sighed. Mr. Westland would return and then she would be alone with him in the alcove. The open balcony doors, thirty feet to her right, beckoned. She could cool off outside for a moment or two, then return before Mr. Westland made it back.

She wound her way through the crowd and out onto the balcony, which she was surprised to find deserted save for a couple who occupied a bench in the shadows of the far corner.

At her appearance, they rose and hurried down the half dozen steps onto the lawn. She sat on the bench in the shadows to the left of the door, near the railing, and watched until the couple were silhouettes beyond the ballroom lights, and then disappeared amongst the darker shadows of trees and bushes.

Lady Claire had said that Grey promised her a walk in the gardens. Jeanine hadn't seen him since their dance. Had he taken Lady Claire for that walk? Maybe they still lingered in the gardens. She breathed deep of the fresh air. The night was warm, but cooler than the stuffy ballroom. Maybe Grey would take her for a walk.

So far, she hadn't met a single gentleman who suited her purposes. How long could she remain Grey's ward if she didn't find a proper husband soon? He said he would help her. That had to mean he would send her home until he found her a suitable husband, as he'd promised. Had he an elderly gentleman in mind? When she thought about it, it wasn't surprising that an elderly gentleman wasn't at the ball. How could a gentleman that old attend a ball? Well, perhaps he could, if he remained seated. But that would be no fun at all.

Tomorrow, she would ask Grey about his plans. Jeanine thought about Miss Stone. What would happen to her once she married? Jeanine would have to bring her to her new household. She couldn't allow her to leave without a good position, because too many employers mistreated companions.

A man and woman emerged from the ballroom. Jeanine's gaze lingered on the lady's dark blue satin dress. She planned to ask Mrs. Morgan if she could make a dress of that color for Miss Stone.

The couple slowed, and the woman said, "Did you see them on the dance floor—and after the way he was carrying on with Lady Claire?"

Jeanine's mind snapped to attention.

"The Morning Star is a master of deceit," she said. "That girl cannot be an innocent."

Jeanine jumped to her feet. "How dare you say such a thing."

The man and woman whirled.

Jeanine stalked to where they stood. "His lordship was perfectly proper with me."

The woman's eyes widened and she glanced at the man, who said, "You misunderstand, my dear."

"I didn't misunderstand anything. G-Grey has been very proper, he even held me at arm's length on the dance floor—which you would have noticed if you weren't so spiteful."

The woman gasped. "How dare you?"

"How can you tell such horrid lies?" Jeanine demanded.

"They aren't lies," the woman spat. "Everyone knows the Morning Star is the worst sort of man."

"D-don't call him that, you mean woman."

The woman's eyes shifted past Jeanine and a male voice drawled, "How very pleasant it is to find you here on the balcony, Lord Fletcher." The marquess halted beside Jeanine. "You're looking lovely, Lady Fletcher. I have been hoping for the opportunity to thank you both for attending tonight's little party."

"It is an honor," Lord Fletcher said. "Thank you for the invitation. However, I believe it is getting late. I must get Margaret home."

The marquess gave a bland smile. "I quite agree."

Lord Fletcher cupped his wife's elbow. "Good night, my lord." He bowed. "Miss Matheson."

They started away. Jeanine turned and watched them reenter the ballroom. "She is a mean and s-spiteful woman," Jeanine said.

"There is no need to excite yourself, my dear," the marquess said.

"But she said awful things about you."

"If I got upset every time someone said awful things about me, I would be upset all the time. "

"Sometimes I d-despise people," she said.

"You are a better person than me," he said. "I despise them all the time. Come, let us sit." He urged her back to the bench where she'd been sitting and lowered himself onto the seat as she sat.

"Why are people so cruel?" she asked.

"The reasons are far too numerous to name and not worth our time," he replied. "Lady Fletcher has a love of gossip and isn't above creating a juicy story if no real tale exists."

"I know," Jeanine said. "She lied outright about you."

"It isn't the first time someone lied about me, and will not be the last. In fairness, Lady Fletcher is not wholly to blame. I invite gossip by living as I please without regard for *Society*."

"That only means you are courageous," she said.

His brows shot up. "How, may I ask, came you to this conclusion?"

She waved a dismissive hand toward the open doors. "They are sheep who follow what *Society* dictates because they do not have the courage—or intelligence—to think for themselves. They are jealous that you do as you please, so they lie to salve their egos."

He stared at her, a strange light in his eyes. "Just the other day, I was told you aren't a grown woman."

"Who said that?" she demanded.

He laughed. "My dear, you are contrary."

Lady Guilford emerged from the ballroom and glanced around the balcony. When her gaze landed on them, she hurried to the bench. "There you are, Jeanine. You are to dance with Mr. Ross soon."

Jeanine shook her head. "I don't want to dance anymore tonight."

"You promised him a dance."

His lordship stood. "If you promised Mr. Ross a dance, then you must dance with him."

"I don't feel like dancing."

His gaze locked with hers. "A lady does not break her promise without good reason."

"I have a good reason. I am angry."

That is *not* a good reason." His expression hardened. "Lady Guilford has worked hard to make this soiree a success. You will not disgrace her *or* me."

Jeanine jumped to her feet. "I would never do that."

"I'm relieved to hear you say so."

"I will not give those scorpions a reason to say anything bad about you on my account." Jeanine grasped his hand. "You believe me, don't you?"

Startlement flickered through his eyes before he gave a gentle smile. "Aye, lass. I believe you. Now, go with my cousin and do as she asks. She knows best what to do at parties like this. An old bachelor like me, I am too out of practice."

She released his hand and snorted. "You may say that all you like, but I am not fooled. You danced with me better than anyone else I danced with tonight."

He laughed. "Go, before I decide that my ward deserves a beating."

She grinned. "You would never do that. But I will go."

CHAPTER 10

JEANINE REENTERED THE BALLROOM WITH LADY GUILFORD AND realized the orchestra was playing a country dance. A good stroke of luck that. At least the dance she would share with Mr. Ross would not be a shorter dance. Lady Guilford slipped along the wall and halted at the corner of the ballroom near the hallway leading to the refreshments table, and scanned the still crowded room.

"We may not find him in time for the next dance," she said more to herself than Jeanine.

Jeanine watched the dancers, suddenly irritated by the loud murmur of voices. She'd never attended a party this large back home. A party with more than a hundred people would have been considered a huge success.

The marquess reentered the ballroom and Jeanine wished that she could dance with him again. He really was a much better dancer than any other partner she'd danced with. She forgot to ask if he had found an elderly gentleman for her.

Lady Claire stepped up behind him and touched his arm. He turned and Jeanine glimpsed his smile when he saw the lady. She leaned close—too close for propriety—and said something. Jeanine couldn't discern his expression, but he leaned a little closer.

"Does Grey know Lady Claire well?" she asked Lady Guilford.

Lady Guilford looked in the direction Jeanine stared. "Well enough," she replied. "Lady Claire's brother is in negotiations with Valan for her hand in marriage."

Jeanine looked sharply at her. "They are to be married?"

Lady Guilford again scanned the ballroom. "Where is Mr. Ross?"

"I didn't know that Grey was to marry," Jeanine said.

"He wouldn't say anything. He is an intensely private man." She laughed. "Despite the fact that he constantly flaunts his improprieties to society. But there is a method to that madness."

"What do you mean?" Jeanine said

Lady Guilford cast her a side glance. "Never mind."

"When will they marry?" Jeanine asked.

"No contract has been signed, and if Valan doesn't take care for his reputation, her brother will retract the offer."

"But he is a marquess—and an earl—not to mention, he is very wealthy. Why would her brother do that?"

"Even a title and money does not save a man from closed doors, if he goes too far. Three years ago, Lord Ingers married a bastard girl barely out of the schoolroom. He found all doors closed to him. He moved to the country and, three years later, his young wife ran off with a navy captain. He never returned to *Town*."

"That could never happen to Grey," Jeanine said. "He is too... too intelligent to let that happen."

"Lady Claire's family does not need a title or money. An alliance must be without reproach," Lady Guilford said. "In truth, I am surprised the family is interested in the connection. Though, ours is a very old family."

Janine started to ask if Grey wanted to marry her, but stopped when he smiled down at Lady Claire. He certainly acted like a man who might consider marriage. What would happen if they married before Jeanine found an elderly gentleman to marry? Would Grey send her away? If his new wife wanted it, yes.

Two dances later, Jeanine decided she really had danced enough for one evening. The gentlemen were polite enough, but they were too young—they would live at least twenty years, maybe thirty—and she'd heard more than enough about new jackets, new horses, and how pretty her eyes were to last a lifetime. She hadn't seen Miss Stone in over an hour. Perhaps she had been smart enough to slip away. Jeanine scanned the ballroom as best as her diminished height would allow, but found no sign of Miss Stone. Perhaps she could slip away too. But she discarded the idea as quickly as it formed, for she knew that Grey would not be pleased, as the party was held in her honor.

She turned to the right to find Miss Stone two steps away. "Miss Stone," she said when her companion reached her, "I've never been so happy to see anyone in my life."

"I am flattered, Miss Matheson. But, surely, you have spoken with many people far more interesting than me tonight."

Jeanine shook her head. "You couldn't be more wrong. Most of the people I spoke with are very dull."

"I find that hard to believe," Miss Stone whispered. "Tonight's guests are among *Society's* most elite. They are highly educated."

"Educated about pretty clothes and horses." Jeanine snorted.

"Oh, and food. I have never met so many people obsessed with food."

"One must know good food in order to entertain," Miss Stone pointed out.

Jeanine sent her a deprecating look. "You're being too kind. I think—" She broke off when two young ladies bypassed a nearby group of men, their eyes on Jeanine.

They stopped in front of her. She had met the girls earlier in the evening, but couldn't recall their names. A frantic search of memory failed to provide any trace of their names.

"Miss Smith." Miss Stone angled her head toward the girl on their left. "Lady Bethany." Miss Stone looked at the other girl then curtsied, and Jeanine could have kissed her.

The two girls acknowledged Miss Stone with a bare nod, then looked at Jeanine as Miss Smith said, "Bethany is hosting a card party tomorrow afternoon. You simply must come."

"Tomorrow afternoon?" Jeanine repeated, and Lady Bethany nodded.

"Do say you will come," Bethany said.

Their eyes remained fixed on Jeanine, as if Miss Stone didn't exist.

"I *adore* cards," Jeanine adopted the same exaggerated, cultured tones the girls used. "We would be delighted to come."

They blinked in surprise.

"We?" Lady Bethany repeated.

Jeanine nodded with exaggerated enthusiasm. "Oh yes, Miss Stone is a wonderful Pharo player."

"Pharo?" the girls said in unison, then exchanged a glance.

"Lord Northington will be pleased to hear that I'm getting out," Jeanine went on as if not noticing their discomfort. "Just yesterday, he commented that Miss Stone and I must accept more invitations."

"Of course," Lady Bethany quickly agreed, and Jeanine had to force back a disgusted roll of her eyes. "I am so pleased you can come," Lady Bethany went on with the same sickening fervor.

Jeanine curtsied. "We are pleased to accept, my lady."

Irritation flicked in the girl's eyes, but she smiled brightly. "Wonderful. I will send round my direction in the morning."

Lady Bethany turned, and Miss Smith followed like an obedient lap dog. They halted as a group of elderly matrons strolled past and Miss Smith said to Lady Bethany in a loud whisper, "Of all the nerve, inviting *her*."

"It was all I could do to remain civil," replied Lady Bethany.

Jeanine looked sharply at Miss Stone, who seemed oblivious to the insults. That was impossible, however. Miss Stone was too intelligent not to know the malicious creatures were referring to her. Jeanine took a step toward them, then halted when Miss Stone grasped her arm.

"I cannot allow you to get into trouble on my account," Miss Stone whispered.

"They deserve to be lashed," Jeanine hissed back.

"Perhaps," Miss Stone replied, "but you mustn't allow them to goad you into doing something that will embarrass you."

"You can't expect culture from a country girl," Lady Bethany said.

Miss Stone took two quick steps to where the girls stood, backs to them. Her slippered toe appeared from beneath her skirt and tamped down on the hem of Miss Smith's satin dress.

"There you are, Miss Stone."

Jeanine whirled to the left at the soft drawl of the marquess's voice. He smiled at her, then turned his attention to Miss Stone, who now faced him, hands clasped before her.

The elderly ladies passed, and the two girls began walking, oblivious to the near ruin of Miss Smith's dress.

"I must compliment you on your pink slippers, Miss Stone," his lordship said.

Miss Stone smiled serenely. "Thank you, sir, but Mrs. Morgan sewed them. All credit must go to her."

"I see. Perhaps I will ask Mrs. Morgan to sew another pair."

"That is too kind of you, my lord, and unnecessary. These are sufficient."

"Aye," he replied. "But you need a pair that doesn't have a mind of their own."

JEANINE SERIOUSLY PONDERED ESCAPE. SURELY, IN THESE WEE hours of the morning, Grey could not fault her for going to bed. Thankfully, some guests had left, but two-thirds remained. One might think they vied for the right to boast that they were the last to leave the Marquess of Northington's party.

"I was hoping to have a moment alone with you."

Jeanine turned at the sound of Lord Gordon's voice.

"You are looking well," he said. "How clever of you to keep up such a brave face."

If ever there was a reason to escape, Lord Gordon provided that reason.

He smiled down at her. "Soon, this will all be over, and I will have you safely out of his reach."

She must be very tired. The man was speaking gibberish. "What will be over?"

He gave her a pitying look. "You are such a sweet innocent." He cupped her elbow and urged her back toward the wall, away from a cluster of nearby ladies. "You may put your faith in me," he whispered. "I have set a plan into motion that will cast him out of *Society* for good."

Her mind snapped to attention. "I beg your pardon?"

"This is not the first time I have saved an innocent from his clutches," he went on.

Her heart began to pound. "What do you mean?"

He hesitated, though she sensed his hesitation was intended

to achieve dramatic effect. It took all her willpower not to seize his shoulders and shake the words from him.

"Of course, you wouldn't have heard," he said. "You were not yet born when *The Morning Star* cast his spell upon the first of his notable victims. Since then, he has made a career of ruining innocents like yourself."

A righteous fervor lit his eyes, and Jeanine refrained from shrinking away.

"At least I was able to save that young woman from a life of ruin." He gave a bitter laugh. "He actually told the poor girl that he wanted to marry her. Can you imagine? The Morning Star in love?"

"What did you do?" Jeanine whispered.

The light in his eyes vanished and he blinked as if startled by her presence. "I have frightened you." He grasped her hand and squeezed. "Forgive me. Let us not speak of this again. Rest easy that he shall not have you." He released her hand and started to turn away, then hesitated as if caught in some terrible inner battle. He looked at her. "I will save you. I only pray that when all is revealed, you will understand why I had to take such drastic measures."

"What drastic measures?" she demanded, but he hurried past the group of ladies.

Jeanine froze for an instant, heart pounding, then started after him. She had to know what he intended. She skirted the ladies, then passed another, smaller group of younger ladies and slowed. He was nowhere in sight.

"Look, she's even chasing after him," a woman whispered behind her.

Jeanine slowed.

"I have it on good authority that she and the marquess were caught together in his library with her kneeling between his legs."

Titters went up.

"That is scandalous, even for the marquess," said another girl.

Jeanine started to face them, then caught herself. She could not make a scene in the ballroom. Grey had been very specific in saying she was not to disgrace him.

Her heart twisted. She could think of only one way to ensure she didn't disgrace him.

CHAPTER 11

VALAN ENTERED THE BREAKFAST ROOM THE FOLLOWING MORNING to find Jeanine staring at her ham and eggs.

She looked up. "Good morning, sir."

Valan lifted a brow as he took his place at the head of the table. "Sir? I have never known you to be so formal at home." He picked up the pot of coffee and filled his cup. "Are you ill?"

Jeanine frowned. "What? Oh, nae. I just—" She hesitated. "I suppose I am still in the mindset of last night's party, surrounded by so many strangers."

Valan forked a slice of ham from the platter and spooned eggs onto his plate. "Did you enjoy the party?"

She nodded. "Of course. It was very gay, was it not?"

"I suppose it was," he said. "But you don't sound enthused."

She smiled, though the smile didn't reach her eyes. "I am just a little tired. It was a great deal of excitement."

"That it was," he agreed. "What plans have you for today?" He took a sip of coffee, then nodded toward the tray of invitations sitting near the edge of the table between them. "It looks as though you and Miss Stone have become much sought after."

Her eyes snapped onto the tray and her expression darkened. "We were invited to a card party. By Lady Bethany. Today."

Valan buttered a triangle of toast. "I assume you will attend?"

"Yes, I would like to attend very much—with Miss Stone, of course."

Valan angled his head in agreement. "Of course. It would be quite rude to leave Miss Stone at home while you attended a party."

Relief flooded her expression. "That is exactly what I thought."

"Is Miss Stone amenable to going?"

"She wasn't, at first. I told her it was only fair that she go with me. You said it would be rude to leave her home," Jeanine added. "But that is the same thing, don't you agree?"

"I agree wholeheartedly," he said. "Miss Stone must surely accompany you." He would give five hundred pounds to see Lady Bethany's face when Jeanine arrived with Miss Stone.

Jeanine gave him a real smile. "I am so glad you agree. Now, Miss Stone cannot refuse to go with me."

"Do you think she would have refused?"

She nodded, then quickly added, "But not because she is stubborn, you understand. She is very aware of propriety—too much so, if you ask me—and she did not want to attend a party where she might be intruding."

"Miss Stone could never intrude," he said, and sipped more coffee.

"That's exactly what I told her. Anyone who thinks differently, well, they deserve what they get."

Valan cut his ham. "What might they get?"

Her gaze sharpened. "I don't know, exactly. But I'm sure it would be unpleasant."

"Just remember, my dear, that the unpleasantness that

happens to people who deserve those things, should be dished out by unpleasant people. Not young ladies."

Her eyes widened in surprise, then a twinkle animated the blue orbs, and he was oddly relieved. "Must you take the fun out of everything, Grey?"

He should have been insulted. Instead, he experienced relief that she called him by name. "Forgive me, my dear, but I feel I must. If only to keep my own neck out of the noose."

The twinkle abruptly vanished and her expression clouded over. "You are right, of course." She returned her attention to her food and seemed to consider, then said, "I believe I have changed my mind, I do no' want to attend the card party."

"Really?" he said. "Only a moment ago, you were excited at the prospect. What has changed in so short a time?" He forked eggs into his mouth and chewed.

She stabbed a bit of ham, moved it to the opposite side of her plate, and used a knife to free it from the tines. "Playing cards is a bore, don't you think?"

"I didn't think so when you won at commerce two weeks ago."

"That is very different. Playing cards, gambling with gentlemen, is far more interesting than playing piquet with ladies who don't truly understand the game."

He would have trouble arguing with that logic. "Perhaps, but there will be a luncheon, maybe a walk in the garden, and even gossip. You cannot tell me that you do not like gossip."

Her head snapped up, and he was startled at the fear in her eyes. "I detest gossip." She laid down her fork. "I am finished with breakfast." She pushed back her chair and rose.

Valan opened his mouth to remind her that a lady always excused herself before leaving a room, but stopped short when he glimpsed a shimmer of moisture in her eyes an instant before she turned and hurried from the room. He leaned back in his chair, staring at the doorway, his mind on last night.

THE CARRIAGE APPROACHED THE HOME AND JEANINE WAS surprised at the size of the mansion. "Lord Gordon's home is larger than Grey's," she said to Miss Stone. "I imagined that Grey had more money than him."

"The size of a man's house does not necessarily indicate his true wealth," Miss Stone said. "His lordship is a man of genteel taste. He will not flaunt his wealth. I am not certain the same can be said of Lord Gordon."

"I suppose you are right," Jeanine said. Lord Gordon certainly didn't have Grey's manners.

The carriage stopped, then tilted to the right as the footman left the perch beside Mr. Potts and descended to the cobblestone. He opened the door and helped them down. Half a dozen other carriages lined the street.

"We will wait here for you, Miss," Mr. Potts said.

"Jeanine smiled up at him. "Thank you, Mr. Potts."

She and Miss Stone started up the walk.

"I must advise against your course of action once more, Miss Matheson," Miss Stone murmured. "I feel certain his lordship can deal with Mr. Gordon."

Jeanine shook her head. "He will advise us to ignore Lord Gordon. I cannot allow Grey's reputation to be blemished on my account. If he wishes to marry Lady Claire, then we must help him."

"I find it difficult to believe he wants to marry her," Miss Stone said.

"Lady Guilford said they discussed marriage negotiations. Men don't enter into marriage negotiations if they don't want to be married."

They reached the door and it opened before they could knock. A somber butler led them down the hallway and upstairs to the first floor. Jeanine spotted servants' stairs to her left as they passed. Two doors down, they reached a parlor and entered.

Jeanine blinked against the glare of the room's bright purples and blues. "My goodness," she blurted, then looked at Miss Stone, whose expression remained bland. Only the hint of disdain in her dark eyes gave away her true feelings. Miss Stone was right. Lord Gordon's taste was not as refined as Grey's.

Two dozen people occupied the room, some at cards tables, some sitting on divans and chairs drinking tea, chatting.

"Miss Matheson." Lord Gordon approached from her right.

Jeanine smiled, and hoped her shock at seeing a bright yellow waistcoat beneath his jacket wasn't obvious. She forced her eyes to meet his and not linger on the ridiculously complex cravat that hung halfway down his chest. He reached them and grasped her hand, then pressed his lips to the back of her hand.

She froze the smile on her face and said, "You remember Miss Stone?"

He bowed, but didn't take Miss Stone's hand. "Of course. A pleasure to see you again, Miss Stone." The words were proper, but Jeanine caught frustration in his voice.

He led them to a table, ordered a maid to bring tea and cake, then launched into inane chatter about the weather, food, and upcoming parties, until Jeanine wanted to scream. She had to break free of him and have a look around the house.

"The ball last night was quite fantastic," he said.

Jeanine nibbled on cake and nodded. "Lady Guilford's efforts made the party an enormous success."

"Indeed," he said. "Indeed. Do you play cards, Miss Stone?"

"No more than passably, sir. Miss Matheson is the expert card player."

"Lady Melanie has despaired of being able to find players. Perhaps you would oblige and play with her."

"As I said, sir, I play only a passable game. I doubt I would offer any challenge."

"But you would," he said. "Lady Melanie is a new player, so could use a patient player like yourself to lend guidance."

"I regret that I must decline," Miss Stone said. "I must remain with my charge."

"Nonsense," Jeanine said. "You have nothing to fear by leaving me to play cards. I will be nearby with Lord Gordon."

Lord Gordon puffed out his chest like a ridiculous peacock. "There you have it, Miss Stone." He rose. "Let me introduce you to Lady Melanie."

Miss Stone glanced at Jeanine, and Jeanine noted genuine concern in her expression. This was the first time she and Miss Stone had disagreed. Shame wormed its way through her. Miss Stone's concerns were founded.

"I must remind you, Miss Matheson, that his lordship instructed us to return after one hour."

A total lie, and one Jeanine hadn't prepared for.

Miss Stone looked at Lord Gordon. "You will forgive us if we don't stay long. His lordship has dinner plans, and allowed us to leave only after extracting the promise that we would not be late."

Irritation flashed in his eyes and he said in a too-genial voice, "Of course, Miss Stone. I shall make it my mission to escort you to your carriage within the allotted hour."

Miss Stone rose, albeit, Jeanine knew, with reluctance, and accompanied Lord Gordon to a table in the far corner of the room near the balcony. The young lady at the table looked to be barely out of the schoolroom. As soon as Lord Gordon turned his back, Jeanine rose and hurried to the door through which they had entered. She slipped from the room, found the hallway empty, and sprinted in the direction they'd come. A second later, she reached the servants' stairs and bounded up the winding staircase.

Light spilled around a curve up ahead. Heart pounding, Jeanine raced up the final stairs and burst into a well-lit hallway. She halted, breathing hard, and strained to hear above the rush of blood in her ears. She saw no one. Not surprising. This had to be Lord Gordon's private chambers. At this time of day, servants might not be allowed on this floor, and most were likely busy with the party.

She tried three doors, found a bedchamber she assumed was Lord Gordon's, but nothing to indicate what he'd meant when he told her he had a plan to cast Grey out of *Society* for good. The next door opened to a private study. She headed for the large mahogany desk at the far end of the room. She had been away from the card room fifteen, maybe twenty minutes. By now, Lord Gordon would believe she had left—or perhaps gone to the garden, if he had one. Miss Stone would have joined the search for her. It was unlikely he would think she'd come upstairs, but anxiety knotted her stomach, nonetheless.

She sat down at the desk and began searching through drawers, but found only paper, pen, personal correspondences that seemed meaningless, and business papers concerning properties he held in the north of Scotland. She opened the bottom right drawer and found several envelopes bound together by a ribbon. Jeanine slid aside the bow that covered the center of the top envelope and started at sight of Grey's first name on the envelope.

With shaking fingers, she tugged the bow free, then untied the ribbon and withdrew the top letter from its envelope.

My dearest Valan,

As usual, I find it easier to put down on paper the words I cannot say. Since becoming your ward, my life had taken on new meaning. It matters not to me what the future holds, so long as we are together. I care nothing for what Society says. I am yours as long as you will have me.

Yours,

Jeanine

Her heart pounded so fiercely, she became lightheaded. She opened a second letter written in a different hand.

My darling Jeanine,

Forget Society. They have never been a friend of mine. I will take you away from here where no one will know us. Never fear, I will not allow harm to come to you or the child you carry... Our child.

Yours forever, Valan

Our child?

Anger twisted through her. She hadn't written these letters. Since she hadn't written these letters, it only made sense that Grey hadn't written the others. And the child that she carried? There was no child. They had never…

Lies. Terrible, vicious lies.

She remembered Lady Fletcher and the girls who had spoken so ill of her and Grey. How many lies were being told about Grey? Now this? But why this?

Then she understood. Lord Gordon had created these terrible lies with the intention of ruining Grey. But why? No one would believe them. Miss Stone lived with them. She could attest to how proper their household ran.

She was not with child. That would prove these were lies. But Grey's reputation would be destroyed before anybody knew they were lies. A mixture of rage and fear brought tears to her eyes. She would not let Lord Gordon do this.

Jeanine quickly gathered the letters and retied the bow. Grey would know what to do. She stood, then hesitated. She couldn't give him the letters. He would be furious. Not because Lord Gordon tried to ruin him, but because Lord Gordon's plan would have ruined her. She didn't know him well, but that much she did know.

The letters had to be destroyed. But that wouldn't be enough, she realized with rising panic. Lord Gordon would only write more. How could she stop him?

She swiped at a tear.

She couldn't. Jeanine thought of Lady Claire. Grey wanted a respectable marriage. She couldn't allow anything to get in his way, even her.

She hurried toward the door. Two steps from the door, it opened. Jeanine came to an abrupt halt. Lord Gordon stood in the doorway. His eyes dropped to the letters she held.

He stepped inside the room and closed the door. "The entire household is searching for you. It never occurred to me you might be here." He took a step toward her and she retreated. He stopped. "There is no need to be afraid. Remember what I told you, that I hoped you would understand why I had to do what I did?"

Jeanine said nothing.

"I will care for you. You will never want for anything. I will marry you."

"M-Marry me?" Jeanine shook the letters in front of her. "I will b-be ruined."

He frowned. "Do you have a speech impediment?"

"Aye. You cannot want a woman who s-stutters."

His frown deepened. "We can deal with that later."

Her mind raced. "I will be ruined. Surely, you c-cannot want to marry a woman whose reputation was ruined by the Marquess of Northington."

"Northington will be blamed," he said. "He is not called *The Morning Star* for nothing. People will understand, and they will draw you into their hearts once you have married me."

"I will no' m-marry you," she spat.

He smiled in what she knew was meant to be comforting, but the effect was undone by the anger that blazed in his eyes. "You do not understand. I know what's best."

Jeanine straightened. "I wish to leave."

He went to a small table beside the door, opened the drawer and withdrew a key. Jeanine watched in horror as he closed the drawer, then locked the door and slipped the key into the front pocket of his waistcoat.

He faced her. "This is for your own good."

He advanced. Jeanine backed up. The back of her leg bumped something. She leapt aside and glanced at the table she'd bumped. She'd retreated nearly to the hearth. From the corner of her eye, she glimpsed the poker resting against the brick. Her heart leapt into her throat. She yanked her gaze back on to Lord Gordon. He stood a foot away.

"Miss Matheson—Jeanine—you need not fear me." He halted. "I understand. Forgive me, dearest. Northington has mistreated you and now you fear all man. I promise, I will be gentle. Come," he grasped her arm.

She started to pull away, then another plan struck. Jeanine tripped and collided with Lord Gordon. She seized his cravat in an effort not to fall—he wasn't quick as Grey had been in catching her—and slipped her fingers into the front pocket of his waistcoat. She fisted the key as he grasped her shoulders.

She thought he would set her back from him, but his hold tightened, and she realized he intended to kiss her. Revulsion turned her stomach. Could she pretend to like the kiss? Wait, he believed she was afraid of Grey. His mouth neared hers. She whimpered.

He froze. "He really has hurt you." The dangerous light of fanatical righteousness flared in his eyes. But, to her relief, he released her. "Sit down." He indicated the nearby chairs. "I will fetch you a sherry. It will be good for your nerves."

He turned, and Jeanine gauged the distance to the door. It was too far. She could never reach it and unlock the door before he set upon her. She would not allow him to trap her. If she didn't escape, then his plans to ruin Grey would succeed. She looked at the poker leaning against the brick of the hearth. Dare she?

"We can live in France, until the worst of the scandal dies

down," he went on. "Have you ever been to France? You will love it."

Jeanine edged to the poker and snatched it up. He filled the first sherry glass, then a second. She had little time. He replaced the lid on the decanter. Jeanine took three steps and lifted the poker with her right hand, while clutching the letters and the key in the other. She swung at his head. He cried out and dropped the sherry glasses. They shattered against the sideboard.

Jeanine dropped the poker and stumbled back two paces. He grabbed the side of his head and swung toward her. She whirled and lunged for the door. Hard fingers seized her arm. She cried out. His fingers dug deeper. He yanked her toward him and she brought her fisted hand up. He grabbed for her and caught the letters. She yanked them free from his grasp. The key struck the carpet.

She stumbled backward as he fell against a chair. Jeanine dove for the key, scooped it up, then raced for the door. Her hands shook so badly she feared she couldn't fit the key into the lock. A moan behind her caused her to glance over her shoulder. He was struggling to his feet. She faced forward, commanded calm, thrust the key into the lock, then turned. The lock clicked. She threw the door open and raced down the hall to the servants' stairs.

She forced herself to slow enough not to fall headlong down the corkscrew stairs. At the bottom, she raced toward the parlor. A shout went up in that direction. Jeanine whirled in the opposite direction and pumped her legs faster. She reached the stairs they had ascended when the butler had shown them in and descended as quickly as she could.

At the bottom, she spun left, toward the front door. Pounding footfalls on the front steps sent her into a panic. She turned right, ran down another hallway that twisted around, and burst into a storage room. Folded linens lined the high shelves. Sacks of fruit and barrels of oats, or maybe flour, encircled the room. She hurried through the small room and nearly cried aloud at sight of a side door. She found the door unlocked, and raced outside into an enclosed garden. Jeanine kept going toward the wooden door on the left side of the stone wall.

Please do not be locked, she prayed. She reached the door, drew the latch, and raced into the alley.

CHAPTER 12

ONE LEG CROSSED OVER THE OTHER AND AN ARM STRETCHED along the top edge of the divan, Valan stared at the emerald ring he wore as he listened to Peigi ramble on about last night's party.

"I had no opportunity to tell you that she invited Lord Gordon," she said. "Of course, with so many last-minute preparations, I then forgot until I saw him enter the ballroom. He had her cornered. I vow, Valan, he all but made violent love to her."

Valan lifted an eyebrow. "I suggest, my dear, that, if you think Jeanine would allow Lord Gordon to make violent love to her in public, that it has been some time since Richard has made violent love to you.

She stiffened. "I beg your pardon. Richard makes violent love to me on a regular basis. I tell you, Lord Gordon was unacceptably fervent."

"Lord Gordon is often fervent," Valan reminded her.

"I don't like it by half," she said. "I wouldn't be one bit surprised to discover that he is trying to talk her into running off with him."

Valan noticed a scuff on one boot. He would have to have a talk with Baldwin.

"Are you listening, Valan?"

He straightened and picked up his teacup from the table. "Of course. I don't think we have to worry about Jeanine running off with Gordon." He sipped his tea, then rested the cup on his leg and leaned back against the cushion.

"What if he attempts to force her?"

He laughed. "I doubt he has the courage."

"That meeting in the park was no accident," Peigi said. "He asked if he could call on her."

Valan chuckled, the imagined scene vivid in his mind's eye. "What was my ward's response to his advance?"

"She didn't respond. I informed him that he must speak with you."

Valan looked sharply at her. "I appreciate your concern, Peigi, but you might allow Jeanine to speak for herself next time."

She frowned. "Next time? You think he will ask again?"

"I think he cannot help himself."

"You would let him court her?" Peigi demanded. Then before he could answer, she added, "So that's your game. This is low, even for you, Valan."

"What is low even for me?" he asked.

"Using the girl to get even with Gordon. That pistol incident happened twenty years ago. Even you should have forgotten it by now."

"Do you think so?" he asked. "I feel certain Gordon has not forgotten."

Peigi regarded him in that way women do when they are puzzling something out about a man, which that man would rather they didn't know. "Perhaps the girl is using *you*."

"Do you really think so?" He considered. "That would be a novel experience."

Peigi shrugged. "You bought her a whole new wardrobe. She lives here, in one of the most luxurious homes in Edinburgh. She travels in the highest of style. Servants cater to her every whim. Women have used men for far less."

"I cannot contradict you on that matter," he said. "In Jeanine's case, however, she asked for none of it."

Peigi snorted. "Lord, but I wouldn't have guessed in a million years that you could be so naïve."

"Naïve?" he said. "Today is truly a singular day. First, I am being used by a woman, now I am naïve."

"What woman wouldn't love living the lifestyle you've provided?" she asked.

"Why shouldn't she love it?" He sipped more tea, then returned the cup to his leg.

Her gaze sharpened. "I have never seen you like this with anyone."

"Like what?" He laughed.

"What if she develops true feelings for Lord Gordon?"

"Jeanine is far too sensible for that. Besides, she wants an elderly gentleman who is facing his next reward."

"So that she can use his money to open a school for young ladies," Peigi said.

He stared at the teacup, remembering the night in the garden when Jeanine revealed her plan to him. "Quite a plan, don't you agree?" he asked.

"I wish she could return home and marry the young man who's in love with her."

Valan looked up. "What young man?"

"Joshua. He drove her here in his wagon—with her younger sister and brother-in-law as chaperones."

Valan nodded slowly. "Today truly is a singular day. That is an eventuality I hadn't considered. It is, of course, only natural that some young swain back home would have fallen prey to her charms. What do you know of this young man?"

"I gather he is a local farmer. She spoke of life in his cottage, raising his children."

"Most women of her rank aspire to such a life," he murmured. "But not Jeanine."

"Are you certain?" his cousin asked.

"She was very clear on that point," he said.

Peigi shrugged. "I suppose it is of no consequence. I suspect she can't return home."

Valan frowned. "What do you mean?"

"She told me she couldn't return home because her mother has just remarried."

Memory slammed into him of their conversation that night in the garden. *"...my mother decided to remarry, two years ago,"* she'd said. *"They only just married last year, which is why I knew I had to take action."*

"Did your mother teach you not to trust strange men?" he'd asked.

She replied, *"Oh, I learned that on my own—and you usually can't trust those you know, either."*

"Her stepfather," he whispered. If the man had— His teacup shattered. The remaining tea spotted his breeches. He straightened.

"Valan!" Peigi cried. "What in the world?" She snapped her eyes up to his face as he picked up the pieces of the cup. "Are you hurt?" she demanded.

"Nae." He set the pieces of china on the tray, snatched up a napkin, and dabbed at the wet spot on his breeches.

She picked up two pieces of broken china from the floor and set them on the tray beside the others. "I see the idea disturbs you as much as it does me."

He didn't have to ask what she meant. "Aye."

"Do you plan to find her a match?" Peigi asked. "The notion of an elderly gentleman is out of the question."

"I am ashamed to admit that I have given the matter little

thought." He tossed the napkin onto the table, then crossed his legs.

"So, you intend to have your revenge on Lord Gordon, then send her on her merry way?" Peigi asked with uncharacteristic perceptiveness.

He hadn't thought about that, either. It would seem he hadn't quite considered this plan as well as he thought he had. Aye, a truly singular day in more ways than he cared to admit.

"It is best you make her a match before it's too late. Do you not agree?" Peigi asked.

"Too late?" he repeated. "Peigi, her reputation is as safe with me as it would be with you."

She gave a frustrated *humph*. "It isn't that. I heard the whispers behind her back at the party."

He stilled. "What sorts of whispers?"

"You cannot be surprised, Valan. She is a country girl. The ladies in town are not kind to girls of her ilk."

"If, by 'her ilk,' you mean girls who are not obsessed with wearing a new dress to every party and throwing themselves into the path of any eligible man, then, aye, you are right."

Her gaze sharpened on him. "Hmm," she hummed.

The door abruptly swung open and Miss Stone hurried in. Strands of hair had fallen loose of her chignon, making her look younger, and a shadow troubled her usually tranquil eyes. She scanned the room, then stilled when her gaze fell on them. Valan had never seen Miss Stone look anything but serene and well-maintained.

"You have returned from the card party, Miss Stone," he said. "Where is Miss Matheson?"

She hesitated. He'd never seen her hesitate. "I must speak with you, my lord—alone."

"You may speak freely in front of Lady Guilford," he said.

"As you wish, sir. I fear you will turn me out without a

reference. I only ask that, once you find Miss Matheson, that you let me know that she is safe."

Valan dropped both feet to the floor and leaned forward. "You alarm me, Miss Stone. What do you mean by 'once you find her'? Is she lost?"

"Not lost, sir. Kidnapped."

WHEN MISS STONE FINISHED HER STORY, VALAN AGAIN STARED at the emerald ring he wore. "When I said today was a singular day, little did I know how right I was."

"We must go at once to Lord Gordon's home and demand that he return Jeanine to us," Peigi exclaimed.

"That is exactly what he would expect us to do," Valan said grimly.

"You don't mean to leave her with him?" Peigi cried.

"I do not." Valan looked at Miss Stone, who sat on the chair to his left, her hands clasped on her lap more tightly than usual. "You searched for half an hour with no sign of her?" he asked. "Gordon was with you that entire time?"

She nodded. "At least for that time, he could not have been aware of her whereabouts."

Valan nodded. "I wonder that my carriage has not returned. You instructed them to stay there until they saw Jeanine?"

"Aye, my lord." She met his gaze squarely. "Despite her command not to tell you, I should have come directly to you."

"On that point, we are in agreement," he said. "We will leave that for later. First, I would like to know if my carriage is still there. If it is, then Gordon will expect a visit from me." He rose and crossed to the door, then pulled the bell pull.

A moment later, Baldwin appeared. "Please have my bay saddled immediately," Valan instructed. "I shall be ready to leave in fifteen minutes."

Baldwin bowed and left.

"You cannot go alone," Peigi said. "Lord Gordon would love nothing better than to finish what he started twenty years ago."

Valan lifted a brow. "Only an hour ago, you told me that I should have forgotten that incident."

She tsked. "An hour ago, he hadn't kidnapped Jeanine. Oh, how I would like to shoot him myself."

He looked at her in surprise. "Peigi, I have never seen you roused to such passions."

Her brow knit in a deep frown. "You're awfully blasé for a man whose ward has been kidnapped."

"Quite the contrary," he said. "But I plan to save my passions for Gordon."

"Do hurry, sir," Miss Stone said. "I am very afraid that he will hurt her."

"That is unlikely," Valan said. "It is me he wants to hurt."

"Would he go so far as to try and force her to marry him?" Peigi asked, but before he could answer, she added, "I am going with you. My presence will hamper him."

"You surprise me, Peigi."

She gave him a haughty look. "Why? You think I don't have a brain."

"Nae, my dear. I simply seldom see you use it." He started toward the door.

"Should I come, as well, sir?" Miss Stone asked.

"If Peigi comes, you come."

A commotion sounded in the hallway and he reached the door as it was flung open. Jeanine entered, accompanied by Mr. Potts and Baldwin.

"I am sorry, sir," Baldwin said. "Mr. Potts insisted on escorting Miss Matheson to you."

"Begging your pardon, sir," Mr. Potts said, "but the young miss was not agreeable to returning home. Miss Stone was very clear that we should see her home if she came out of Lord Gordon's mansion."

Valan took in the hair that had come loose from Jeanine's soft chignon, her torn sleeve, and a handful of envelopes wrapped in a bow that she gripped. Her mouth was set in a mutinous line.

"When she came out of the alley behind Lord Gordon's house we hurried to pick her up, but she didn't want to come with us," Mr. Potts went on. "We had to force her into the carriage."

Valan looked sharply at him. "Is that when her dress was torn?"

Mr. Potts drew himself up. "We would never harm a hair on the lass' head. She came out of Lord Gordon's home looking like this."

Valan looked at Jeanine. "Is that so?"

"Mr. Potts kidnapped me," she said.

"I was under the impression it was Gordon who kidnapped you," Valan said.

Her lower lip trembled, then fury flashed in her eyes. "He tried to kidnap me. But I brained him with a poker and escaped."

"Brained him with a poker?" Valan repeated in shock.

She nodded.

"Am I to assume you killed him?"

"Unfortunately, his head was too hard for me to kill him that easily."

"I must admit, I am much relieved," Valan said.

"He deserved to be killed," she said with heat.

"I quite agree," Valan said. "Only, you shouldn't be the one to kill him."

Her eyes lit. "Will you kill him, Grey?"

He frowned. Your love of violence concerns me, my dear." He looked at Baldwin and said, "I will not need my bay, Baldwin." Then, to the driver, "I owe you a great debt, Mr. Potts".

"Harry deserves as much credit as I do, my lord."

"Harry?" Valan asked.

"Aye, sir, Harry MacLean, the footman who was with me."

Valan nodded. "It seems I am in both your debts."

"Think nothing of it, my lord." The man bowed and left with Baldwin.

Valan turned to Miss Stone. "I owe you thanks as well, Miss Stone."

"I cannot see how, sir, as it is my fault that Miss Matheson was kidnapped."

"I wouldn't go that far," he said. "I will ask, however, that the next time you two decide upon a scheme, that you speak with me first."

"It isn't her fault," Jeanine said. "I told her not to tell you."

Valan nodded. "The blame lays at your feet, never fear, my dear. But we will discuss that later. For now, I would like you and Miss Stone to go upstairs and rest. We shall have dinner, then go to the opera."

"I don't want to go to the opera," she said.

"I understand you've had trying day," he said. "But I ask that you do me this favor." He looked at Miss Stone. "I would like you to accompany us—and Peigi, if Richard can spare you, I require your presence, as well."

Miss Stone rose and walked to where Jeanine stood. "You are unharmed, Miss Matheson?"

"Aye, he didn't hurt me at all."

Valan's attention caught on the envelopes she held. "What are those?"

She looked down at them as if having forgotten them. "You will no' like it."

"Does that mean they have something to do with Gordon's plot to ostracize me from *Society*?"

Jeanine looked at Miss Stone, hurt in her eyes. "You told."

"Don't blame her," Valan said. "She believed you had been kidnapped. May I have them, please?"

She hesitated. "On one condition."

He waited.

"You will promise not to take action."

"Only a moment ago you wanted me to commit murder."

She looked at the floor. "Aye, but if you did that it would be calculated. After reading these letters, you will be so angry that you might make a mistake." She lifted her eyes to his face. "You…cannot be killed and you cannot be involved in another scandal, if you are to marry Lady Claire."

"Marry Lady Claire?" he blurted. "Where did you get that idea?"

Her eyes widened. "I heard it."

"I have no intention of marrying Lady Claire," he said.

"Her brother isn't in negotiations with you for marriage with her?"

"Her brother has been trying to talk me into marrying her for two years," Valan said.

"You see," Miss Stone said, "I told you he didn't want to marry her."

"But I—"

"Up to your rooms," he cut off Jeanine. She sighed, then started to turn toward the door. "Jeanine." She stopped. "The letters, please."

Fear flickered in her eyes, but she handed them to him and left the room like a woman walking the gallows.

The door clicked closed behind them and Valan returned to his seat on the divan. He pulled the ribbon from the envelopes. "Peigi, I prefer you do not discuss my personal affairs with anyone, Jeanine in particular."

"I am sorry," she said. "It is true, the earl did send you a contract."

"Which I promptly returned unopened—for the third time."

"She cares for you, Valan."

He laughed as he pulled a paper from the first envelope. "Lady Claire cares for herself only."

"I meant Jeanine.

He looked up at her.

"She is protecting *your* reputation."

"Can you imagine?" he said. "An innocent wants to protect *The Morning Star*. I will likely never experience another day like today."

He withdrew the letter from within the first envelope and began reading.

CHAPTER 13

WHEN THEY ENTERED THE OPERA HOUSE, THE FURTIVE GLANCES
and low murmurs told Valan the gossip that Jeanine had
rejected Lord Gordon's suit had spread through Edinburgh
more quickly and thoroughly than he'd hoped. He would have
to thank Peigi. Her network of gossipmongers was impressive.

He kept Jeanine close. Between himself, Miss Stone and
Peigi, she would remain safe. Valan had to admit, he'd never
enjoyed the opera more, and intermission came all too soon.
He ordered refreshments and stood. He was getting to old to
sit for so long without stretching. A knock came to the box
door. The women all looked at him.

He started toward the door.

"Please do not get angry," Jeanine begged.

"What have I to be angry about, my dear?" He opened the
door.

Young Martin Hayes stood outside their box in the dimly lit
walkway. Valan had a good idea what the lad wanted. An unex-
pected sadness stabbed.

"My lord," Martin began.

Valan held up a hand, palm out, and looked over his

shoulder at the women. His attention caught on Jeanine's midnight blue satin dress. The fabric hugged her curves and almost gleamed in the candlelight. Her met her gaze. Fear shone in her eyes.

He smiled gently. "Ladies, excuse me. I will be just outside the door, speaking with Mr. Hayes." He stepped from the room and closed the door.

"My lord, forgive the intrusion," Martin began, then waited as a man and woman passed. When they were out of earshot, he said, "What is this nonsense about my grandfather wedding a young woman?"

"Perhaps you should speak with your grandfather," Valan said.

"I have, but he refuses to give me any details other than you know the lady. Is that true?"

"It is," Valan said.

"Sir, surely you realize my grandfather is quite elderly. What can he possibly want with any wife, much less a young one?"

"Perhaps when you are an old man you will understand," Valan said.

The lad stiffened. "I am a man of the world, and not ignorant of a lady's charms. But my grandfather—bloody hell, sir, she can be of no good use to him, and he certainly cannot be of any use to her."

"You might underestimate your grandfather," he replied mildly, and was startled to realize the thought bothered him.

Martin frowned as if Valan were insane. "I demand that you cease interfering in my grandfather's affairs."

"I would say it is you who are interfering."

"The young lady will not be welcome in our house," Martin snapped.

Valan looked at him through shuttered eyes. "Do you refer to Whitmore House or perhaps Howton Castle?"

The lad's mouth fell open. "Are you saying *we*, his family, would not be welcome in our grandfather's home?"

"I believe that is what you are saying."

A manservant arrived with the refreshments Valan had ordered. He stepped aside and allowed the man entrance, then said to Martin, "You will excuse me. I hope you enjoy the remainder of the opera." Valan angled his head in a slight bow, then returned to the opera box and closed the door.

WHEN THEY FINALLY ARRIVED HOME, JEANINE WASN'T SURPRISED when Grey insisted that Peigi stay the night, as her home was nearly an hour away. She took the Gold guest chambers.

Despite Miss Stone's insistence that she needed to help Jeanine with her evening toilet, Jeanine sent Miss Stone to her chambers. Jeanine sat on the bench at her vanity, her heart filled with a mixture of relief and apprehension. The half dozen prayers she'd sent up during the opera had been answered. Lord Gordon hadn't made an appearance. But she knew too well he wasn't finished with the marquess. Grey said he wasn't to marry Lady Claire, but what if that had been a lie so that she wouldn't feel responsible for the trouble she'd caused?

Either way, Lord Gordon could—and would—ruin him on account of her. Not to mention, Grey was certain to exact revenge for the awful letters Lord Gordon had written. Grey hadn't said a word to her about the letters, but he wouldn't. Lady Guildford was right; Grey was an intensely private man.

Her heart squeezed. She had to leave Finley Hall.

Tomorrow morning, before Grey and Miss Stone arose, she would slip away. Tears pricked. Grey could find some respectable lady to marry. Maybe even Lady Claire. Lady Claire certainly would not want to marry a man who had a full-grown woman as his ward. Jeanine's heart began to beat fast. This meant that when she'd bid Grey good night ten minutes ago, that would be the last time she would see him. Had she known that would be their final goodbye, she would have lingered a moment longer. Would have memorized his face a little better, the cool look in his eyes. She might even have squeezed his hand to feel the warmth of his touch one final time.

Jeanine jumped to her feet and began pacing. Could she really leave without seeing him at least once more? She shook her head. She was simply trying to talk herself out of leaving tomorrow. She had to leave before Lord Gordon had the opportunity to put another plan into action. She swiped at tears and crossed to the small secretary near the bay window. She sat down, pulled out a pen and paper, and penned a short note explaining to Grey that she had returned home and he need not worry.

She hesitated over the signature. Should she say 'Yours, Jeanine?' Or 'Your Friend, Jeanine?' Maybe that was too personal. Maybe she should sign, 'Miss Matheson.' She glanced at her salutation. *Dear Grey.* She couldn't call him Grey then sign as 'Miss Matheson.' She had to sign her Christian name. She considered for another moment, then wrote, *Your Friend, Jeanine.* She folded the note, then stared at it. All that remained was for her to slip away tomorrow morning.

But tomorrow morning was hours away.

Jeanine jumped to her feet. She opened the door and stepped into the hallway, then came to an abrupt halt when Miss Stone rose from the chair on the opposite wall.

"Miss Stone, what are you doing here?"

"Forgive me, Miss Matheson, but I feared you would try to run away. You shouldn't, you know. Lord Northington will deal with Lord Gordon."

Tears pressed the backs of Jeanine's eyes. Where would she

ever find a truer friend? Never. But she couldn't tell her good friend the truth.

Jeanine smiled. "I am still in my gown. I would never run away dressed in an evening gown."

"I am not so certain."

Jeanine laughed. "I cannot sleep. I am just going downstairs to see if Grey is still up. You go to bed and I will see you in the morning." Jeanine started to turn.

"Miss Matheson."

Jeanine stopped.

"I am sorry I deserted you at Lord Gordon's."

"What—you didn't desert me." Guilt assailed her.

Jeanine pulled her into a hug. She thought for an instant she detected a tremble in Miss Stone, but Miss Stone stepped back and stared with her usual composed expression.

"I will see you in the morning," Jeanine said.

"Do you promise?"

She smiled. "I promise."

Miss Stone nodded, and Jeanine went downstairs to Grey's library. She couldn't allow herself to think of Miss Stone, for Grey would guess in an instant that something was wrong. Soft light fanned out beneath the library door. Her pulse jumped. He hadn't gone to bed yet.

She knocked. He called "enter," and she opened the door.

The marquess looked up in surprise. Aside from the modest light from the hallway, the room was lit by only a single candelabra located on the desk where he sat. One of Lord Gordon's letters lay open before him, the others in a stack to his right.

He folded the letter and rose. He had taken off his coat and cravat. The top buttons on his shirt were undone, revealing tanned skin and his sleeves were rolled up to his forearms. A strange tremor rippled through her.

"Is something wrong?" he asked.

Jeanine started to close the door, then remembered that he

had told her she was never to close the door when they were in a room alone together.

She crossed to his desk and said, "I couldn't sleep."

He smiled gently. "So, I see. You're still in your ballgown. It is past time we go to sleep, though, don't you agree."

Her heart fell.

He smiled. "Perhaps a sherry will relax us both."

She smiled in return. "Yes, please."

He poured two sherries, then faced her, glasses in hand. "Shall we sit?"

An idea struck. "Can we play a game of chess?"

He lifted a brow. "You play?"

She nodded. "My father loved to play, but none of my cousins played with him, so he taught me."

Grey approached and handed her one of the glasses of sherry. "Your father sounds like an enlightened man."

She laughed. "It's more likely he was just desperate for someone to play with. I am a fair player."

Grey canted his head. "We can start a game and finish tomorrow, if necessary."

They sat at the game table and set up the pieces. Jeanine felt as if they existed in their own private world with the candle-light enveloping them in soft light while the rest of the room lay in shadow. Grey took the black pieces, of course, and she the white. Jeanine went first, and took her time deciding on the first move. Grey decided his first move more quickly than she did, but she intended to draw the game out as long as possible. Her head slightly bent as if her attention was on the board, she lifted her eyes and studied his serious expression when it came his turn to move.

Twenty minutes into the game, he leaned back in his chair and sipped his sherry, his eyes on her face. "I can see why your father liked playing with you. Was he a good player?"

"Oh yes, much better than me."

"Then he was quite good."

Jeanine moved her knight. "Your turn."

She sipped her sherry. "What are your plans for tomorrow?"

"I have no particular plans. I seldom do."

"Really? But you always seem to be busy," she said

His mouth lifted in a tiny smile. "Do I?"

"What do you do all day?"

"Nothing that would interest you."

She leaned forward. "But it would interest me."

He studied the board a little longer this time.

"Did it please you to take me as your ward?" she asked.

"It did."

"Despite all the trouble I've been?"

He smiled, but kept his attention on the board. "Despite all the trouble you've been." He moved his queen.

"I'm very sorry about the trouble with Lord Gordon."

He looked sharply at her. "That was not your fault."

"But I went to his house and I shouldn't have."

The marquess picked up his sherry glass again and leaned back his seat. "True, you shouldn't have. But Lord Gordon was troublesome long before you came along."

She frowned. "He said something about saving another innocent from your clutches."

Grey's expression darkened. He downed the last of his sherry in one swallow, then rose and crossed to the sideboard. "Did he say anything more?"

"Nae. I asked what he meant, but he was very cryptic. I knew he was lying. He is a terrible person." The memory of his words fired her blood. "I almost wish I had killed him when I hit him with the poker. I wanted to."

Valan returned to his seat. "Be glad you didn't. We might very well have been forced to flee to France or, worse, the Colonies."

She thought of her and Grey in France, attending dances

and drinking coffee every morning. "Would that have been so terrible?"

"Indeed, it would," he said with such conviction that her heart hurt. He must have read her expression, for he said, "Not because I don't enjoy your company, but I would not have you a wanted criminal."

"Really?" she asked. "My company is not so terrible?"

A strange light entered his eyes. "Not so terrible, at all."

"I promise, I will not be any more trouble," she said.

She thought his gaze had shifted to her mouth, then he dazzled her with a bright smile and said, "I can't imagine how you will manage that," and she decided she'd been wrong.

Her heart twisted. This would be the last time she would see that sparkle in his eyes. She ducked her head and looked at the chess pieces. "Thank you for making me your ward. I have been very happy."

"Then I am happy, as well," he murmured in a strange voice.

Jeanine nodded and dared not look at him for fear she would cry. She moved her rook. He reached for his rook, and her gaze fixed on his long fingers as he moved his chess piece across the board in line with her queen.

"Really, Grey," she said with disdain. "That move is too obvious. If I didn't see that I would be a real ninny."

"And you are no ninny."

She pinned him with a stare. "You're planning a trap."

His eyes widened in mock innocence. "Me? Never."

Jeanine studied the board. If her calculations were correct—

A shadow fell across the carpet to her right and she looked up and gasped. Lord Gordon stood in the doorway.

"How very cozy the two of you are," he said with mock sweetness.

The word 'cozy' sounded more like 'coshy.' Was he drunk?

"It seems I was closer to the mark with you two than even I realized," he said.

'Seems' came out 'sheems'

Valan rose. "The hour is late, Gordon. Why are you here?"

Lord Gordon stepped into the room and listed a little to the right. "You know full well why I'm here." The words were more of a drunken growl than English.

"I am distressed that the footman who should've shown you in didn't announce you," Valan said.

"Never mind him," Lord Gordon snapped. "How dare you tell everyone that she rejected *my* suit. You can't stand that I bested you twenty years ago. *The Morning Star*," he sneered the name. "You flout *Society*, yet they welcome you with open arms." His eyes snagged on the letters sitting on the desk. He took two steps to the desk and snatched up the envelopes. "So, your little whore came straight to you." He threw them onto the carpet. "All the better. Servants will whisper about how they saw the letters in your library." His bloodshot eyes swung onto Jeanine. "I thought you were different."

Anger swept through her. She leapt to her feet. "Different from what?"

"I believe he is referring to an old friend of mine," Grey said.

"Old friend, that's rich," Lord Gordon said. "She was just another one of your whores."

"Being drunk is no excuse for being a liar," Grey said in a voice so cold that it sent a shiver down Jeanine's back.

Grey started toward him. Lord Gordon jammed a hand into his coat pocket and whipped out a pistol. Grey froze. Jeanine drew a sharp breath.

Grey stepped in front of her. "Your quarrel is with me, Gordon."

He gave a vicious laugh. "You believe you are so superior to the rest of us." His eyes glittered. "I was there, you know."

"There?" Grey repeated as if they were discussing nothing more than afternoon tea.

"When they found your father."

Jeanine's attention caught on the flex of Grey's hands into fists.

"His death should have finished you," Gordon said with such spite that Jeanine wished she had another poker so that she could brain him again. This time, she would kill him. His mouth twisted upward in a malicious smile. "How does it feel being guilty of the same crime your father's murderer was guilty of? He is a murderer, you know. When Lord Graves won your father's fortune, he might as well have pulled the trigger of the pistol your father used to shoot himself. Did the man whose fortune you won shoot himself, as well?" Lord Gordon stepped toward them. "You've guarded that secret jealously. Who was he?"

"A Frenchman," Grey replied. "You wouldn't know him."

Cold fingers inched up Jeanine's spine. She had the strangest feeling he was lying.

"What do you want?" Grey asked.

"I plan to marry her." He motioned with the pistol in Jeanine's direction.

"I won't marry you," Jeanine exclaimed.

"I imagine you intend to shoot me first," Grey said in a level voice.

He kept the pistol pointed at Grey. "Come here, Miss Matheson, or I *will* shoot him."

"Stay where you are, Jeanine," Grey said. "I am sorry, Gordon, but I cannot allow you to take her."

"How will you stop me? You don't keep a pistol in your house. Can't stomach the sight of them, I understand. The night you climbed into Lady Victoria's bedchambers, you didn't put up even the slightest bit of a fight. The pistols her brother and I pointed at you rendered you helpless as a little girl."

"You won," Grey said. "That isn't enough?"

"She never stopped talking of you," he snarled. "Her brother had to send her away."

"She was fifteen," Grey said. "Girls that age are prone to lovesickness. She married a viscount and has three children."

"She should have been mine," Lord Gordon snapped. "She would have been, but you ruined her."

"I never touched her," Grey said.

"Liar," he hissed. Eyes on Grey, he said, "Come here, Miss Matheson. Defy me, and I'll shoot him."

"You can't possibly get away with this," Grey said.

"On the contrary. You put it about that Miss Matheson rejected me, but when they learn that we married, they'll know that was just spiteful gossip spun by you. *Society* will have to acknowledge that a simple country girl preferred me to *The Morning Star.*"

"I will tell everyone the truth," Jeanine spat.

He gave her a harsh smile. "When we return from France with you heavy with my child, you will be glad for my protection. Unless you really are carrying his child already."

Jeanine lifted her chin. "Grey has been nothing but a gentleman."

"How noble."

Movement in the hallway caught her attention.

Grey took a step toward Gordon.

"Nae," Jeanine cried. "He will shoot you."

Miss Stone lunged through the doorway. Grey dove for Gordon. The gun fired with a deafening roar. Jeanine screamed when Grey stumbled. She sprang forward as Miss Stone collided with Lord Gordon, but felt as if she was struggling through quicksand.

The marquess caught himself and stumbled toward Lord Gordon. Miss Stone raked her nails down Lord Gordon's cheek. He howled and shoved her aside. She hit the carpet and the marquess crashed into him. They fell to the rug with a thud as Jeanine reached them. She leapt aside as the two men rolled across the rug in a death grip.

Miss Stone shoved into a sitting position. Jeanine looked wildly about the room for something to hit Lord Gordon with. Her ears rang. Two men appeared in the doorway. She yanked her gaze up and saw the gentleman she'd met in Grey's library two days ago, Baron Rosemund, along with another tall, dark-haired man.

"What in God's name—" Baron Rosemund rushed to Grey and Lord Gordon.

He dealt a hard kick to the side of Lord Gordon's head with his boot heel. The man went limp. Jeanine rushed to Grey's side and fell to her knees beside him. Blood spotted the sleeve of his left shoulder.

Baron Rosemund nodded toward Lord Gordon. "I assume he is the reason your door is open and a footman is lying unconscious in your foyer?"

The marquess looked sharply at him. "Is the footman dead?"

Brendan shook his head. "Nae. But I'll wager he has a devil of a headache tomorrow."

"What are you doing here?" Grey actually sounded peeved.

"We had a meeting," the baron said.

Grey grunted. "I sent a note, cancelling."

"Anthony insisted on ignoring that," Rosemund said. "You should be grateful he did."

"What the devil is all this about?" the other man demanded.

Jeanine gingerly fingered Grey's wound. "You are bleeding." She dropped onto her backside and pinned him with a hard stare. "I specifically instructed you not to be hurt on my account."

His brows rose. "The bullet barely grazed me." He looked up at the baron. "Brendan, if you would." He extended a hand.

The baron clasped his hand and hauled him to his feet. Grey

reached for Jeanine, but she scrambled to her feet and grabbed his arm.

"You must sit down." Jeanine looked over her shoulder. "Miss Stone, please wake Mr. Baldwin and have him call for a doctor."

Lady Guilford burst into the room with Mr. Baldwin and Mrs. McPhee close behind.

Lady Guilford skidded to a halt, her sleeping cap askew on her head. Her eyes widened and her hand flew to her heart. "What happened? Valan, you're bleeding."

"A mere flesh wound," he said with exasperation.

"Mr. Baldwin," Jeanine said, "please call for a doctor."

Mr. Baldwin glanced at Grey, who sighed and said, "She will not be satisfied until a doctor confirms that I am not dying."

The steward disappeared.

"Mrs. McPhee, will you bring tea for everyone?" Jeanine asked.

The housekeeper looked at Grey. He nodded, and she hurried from the room.

"Very clever of you, my dear," Grey said to Jeanine. "They will stay busy for some time."

"Will someone tell me what is going on?" Lady Guilford demanded. Lord Gordon moaned and she jumped. "Good lord, is that—" Her eyes snapped onto the marquess. "I told you he would go too far."

"As usual, you were right, Peigi."

"We should call for a constable," she said.

"Aye." Grey looked at Baron Rosemund. "Brendan, I would greatly appreciate—"

The baron held up a hand. "Say no more—well, until we return. I will want to hear this story in full."

Grey canted his head. "I would prefer to tell the story but

once. When the constable comes, you and Anthony may hear everything in full."

"Come along, Anthony."

Baron Rosemund grabbed Lord Gordon by his left arm and the other man grabbed his right arm, and they hauled him to his feet. He moaned as they dragged him out the door.

"You must sit down." Jeanine pulled him to the couch and pushed him onto the cushion. "Miss Stone." Jeanine whirled. Miss Stone stood near the desk, hair askew. "Are you unharmed?"

"I am perfectly fine."

"What in the world were you doing in the hall?" Jeanine demanded.

"I feared you weren't being truthful when you said you would see me in the morning."

Jeanine flushed, but said, "Well, I am immensely glad you were there. Will you fetch water and some fresh cloths, please?"

She nodded and hurried from the room. Only Lady Guilford remained.

"Peigi, if you are to hear the story, I suggest you dress," said his lordship. "Brendan and Anthony will no doubt return within an hour accompanied by a constable."

She nodded and left.

Then Grey looked at Jeanine.

CHAPTER 14

VALAN WAS LOATH TO ADMIT THAT EVEN A FLESH WOUND COULD ache. He was getting too old for such nonsense. Despite the fact he had bled only enough to ruin his crisp white shirt, Jeanine was still applying pressure to the 'wound.'

Valan regarded her with a stern eye. "That was foolish of you."

"Me?" She dropped onto the couch beside him, her fingers *still* pressed against the wound. "You are the one who ran straight into the barrel of a pistol."

He grunted. "Gordon has always been a bad shot."

Jeanine's eyes widened, then she burst into tears and buried her head in his chest.

He grimaced when she squeezed his wound. Valan grasped her hand and held it. "Shh, sweet. All is well. I am not really hurt."

"You could have been killed," she wailed.

"I am not so easily killed."

"You would have been better off to have never known me."

His life had been far less complicated before her, quieter, colder...without love.

"Now the scandal will ruin you," she sobbed into his shirt. "You won't be able to marry Lady Claire."

He frowned. "I believe I told you that I had no intention of marrying Lady Claire."

"You just said that to make me feel better."

"I never say things just to make anyone feel better. I have never had any desire to marry Lady Claire."

"You wanted to walk with her in the gardens," Jeanine blubbered.

He laughed. "That is a far cry from wanting to marry someone."

She drew back and turned her tearstained face up to him. "What is wanting to marry someone?"

With the pad of this thumb, he gently wiped tears from her cheek. "Wanting to marry someone is being unable to imagine a day without them."

She straightened. "Oh dear."

He tensed. "What is amiss?"

She looked at her lap and shook her head. With a finger beneath her chin, he tipped her face up toward him. He lifted a brow and waited.

She stared back for a long moment, then sighed. "If wanting to marry someone is not being able to imagine a day without them, then I want to marry you."

Longing twisted through him. "Perhaps there is a bit more to it than that," he said.

"Such as liking to play chess with them? Or..." Her gaze dropped to his mouth and lingered there for two heartbeats, then lifted again to meet his eyes. "Or wanting to kiss them?"

He tweaked a lock of her hair that had come loose of the chignon. "You want to kiss a young man. I am too old for you, my dear."

"That is silly. I said from the start that I wanted an older man."

"You said that you wanted a man with one foot in the grave. I am, I hope, too many years away from that to qualify."

"I do not want you to die," she blurted. "I want—" She looked up at him through her lashes and nibbled on her bottom lip. "I want you to marry me."

He smiled gently. "I do not think that's what you really want."

"It is. You *must* marry me."

He lifted a brow. "Indeed?"

She nodded. "It's the only way to save you from scandal. You know that what happened here tonight will be all over Edinburgh by breakfast."

She was right about that.

"And the story will be twisted to paint you in a very poor light."

She was right about that, as well. "It won't be the first time, and not the last," he replied.

"People marry all the time to save themselves from scandal," she said.

"Perhaps, but I am too far gone to be saved."

She continued to nibble her bottom lip. "Then marry me to save *me* from scandal." He started to reply, but she added, "I cannot return home. My mother's new husband would never allow it."

He wouldn't allow that, anyway. "What of Joshua?" he asked gently.

Surprise flickered in her eyes. "Joshua is kind, but if rumors reach him that I am pregnant with your child…" She shrugged.

Valan pictured Gordon slumped between Brendan and Anthony when they dragged him from the room and was glad he was gone. If the two men hadn't take him away, Valan would kill him. Still…Gordon wasn't wholly to blame.

He looked at Jeanine. "There is no need for you to sacrifice yourself. I have found an elderly gentleman for you to marry."

"You did?" she exclaimed, then frowned. "I do no' care. It's marry you or be ruined."

He laughed. "More experienced women than you have tried to coerce me into marriage."

"I think you mean 'tricked.' I am not tricking you. I am telling you directly that it's marriage or ruin."

Sadness squeezed his heart. "Why would you want to marry me, love?"

She looked at him in surprise. "Because I love you, silly."

Peigi and Miss Stone entered. Peigi wore a soft yellow day dress, and Miss Stone carried a basin and pitcher, and had clean cloths slung over her shoulder. They stopped inside the doorway.

"Marry the elderly gentleman, Jeanine," he urged. "Your comfort will be assured."

She stared up at him, eyes shimmering. "Don't you love me just a little?"

He smiled sadly. "I love you far too much to marry you. I don't deserve you."

"Yes, you do—and I deserve you." She threw her arms around his neck. "Say yes. I promise I will not be one bit of trouble anymore and I will do everything just as you tell me to."

"I don't think you can," he said with a laugh.

She pulled back and looked up at him, her expression serious. "Marry me and I will make certain you are never sorry."

"It isn't me who will be sorry, love."

She tilted her head to one side. "Will you be sorry if you don't marry me?"

"Yes, but that is my penance."

Jeanine stood. "Do you want me to be happy?"

He sighed. "With all my heart."

She held out her hand.

He clasped it and stood.

She looked up into his face. "I cannot imagine life without you."

"It's insanity," he whispered.

Tears glistened in her eyes. "Insanity?" she repeated. "It is insanity to be apart."

He wondered how he would face tomorrow without her bursting into his study with some new gift or a story about Miss Stone.

"You are certain?" he asked. "If we wed, I will not let you go." He wondered if he could let her go if she refused.

Jeanine frowned. "Where would I go?"

Valan crushed her to him and closed his eyes. Something primal twisted in his chest. She loved him. The urge to protect her nearly suffocated him. She didn't need his money, his house…his body.

Him. She wanted him.

He released a deep breath, then loosened his hold on her and looked over her head at his cousin. "Peigi, if you are available, we require your presence three days hence for a wedding."

Peigi clapped her hands. "We must start planning immediately." She turned and frowned at Miss Stone. "Stop gawking, Miss Stone, and see to his lordship's arm before he feigns death in order to escape his own wedding."

Miss Stone started toward him, but Valan dipped his head and kissed his future wife.

SNEAK PEEK AT A MARRIAGE OF NECESSITY

A Marriage of Necessity
The Marriage Maker
Book Eight
Rules of Refinement

Tarah Scott

He offered one night. She needs a lifetime...

When Viscountess Kinsley's father lost all but their home and then drank himself to death, creditors stood ready to seize what remained. Anne's only hope of saving her family is to find a husband through Lady Peddington's School for Young Ladies. Only, upon graduation, Anne finds herself the victim of jealous gossip that claims she seeks multiple lovers. Now, no respectable man will have her.

Kennedy Douglas, Viscount Buchanan, has refused to marry—until his terminally ill father threatens to marry Kennedy's younger sister to a known wife-beater unless Kennedy immediately weds and produces an heir. The man known as The Marriage Maker matches Kennedy with the ravishing Viscountess Kinsely, but time is running out. Kennedy's father is declining rapidly, and he's the only one who knows where Kennedy's sister is being held against her will.

CHAPTER 1

Anne angled away from her best friend, Jeanine, drew back the edge of her glove, and glanced at the face of the silver gilded watch pinned to the inside of the fabric. 11:57. If her watch was correct, and the time piece had kept perfect time for three generations, the third ball of the season would end in three minutes when the minuet concluded. Then Lady Peddington's famed Midnight Ball would begin.

A year of her life, along with funds her family could ill afford to lose, gone. All for nothing, if she didn't find a wealthy husband by the next ball, which was one short week away. Her heart constricted. *Oh, papa, why didn't you tell us?*

She knew why. Her father had been a Weber male through and through. They were stubborn to a fault, determined to care for their own at all costs, and slaves to the gambling halls. In the end, he had the presence of mind to lay down his cards before he lost the castle on Loch Lomond, and the estate and land north of Perth. Her father, however, feared he couldn't resist the temptation to gamble away their remaining holdings and drank himself to death.

The need to cry rushed to the surface.

Nae, the time for despair was long past. She had to—

A tall, dark, good-looking gentleman approached. Anne's mind snapped to attention. Two minutes remained of the respectable ball. It was impossible to join in the dance so late in the set, but would this gentleman engage her in conversation? He continued toward them. Anne turned her attention to Jeanine. It wouldn't do for her to appear too eager.

"I am so glad this ball is almost over," Jeanine said. "It is so hot and stuffy in here. I think there are more guests tonight than last week. I wonder if there will be even more for the final ball of the season."

From the corner of her eye, Anne watched the man's approach. He brushed past a group of men.

"Aye, it is warm tonight," Anne said to Jeanine. "We can go back to our rooms together, if ye like."

The man reached them, and she and Jeanine faced him. He looked at Anne. Her pulse jumped. Finally, a gentleman was going to speak with her. He would be the first of the evening.

Then his attention shifted to Jeanine. "Would ye honor me with a turn around the ballroom?"

Tears stung Anne's eyes. She ducked her head as Jeanine said, "I have tired. But Lady Anne is free. Why don't you walk with her?"

Anne snapped her head up in time to see the man stiffen. "I beg your pardon, but it is getting late. I must be going. Have a good evening." He started to turn.

"Wait," Jeanine cried. The man stopped, interest lighting his eyes. "Why won't you walk with Anne?" Jeanine demanded.

"Jeanine," Anne hissed under her breath, and she glanced at a group of nearby ladies who were frowning in their direction. But Jeanine ignored her.

"Do you know that she's the heir to a title?" Jeanine asked.

"I have no need of a title," he said, and before they could reply, he spun and strode away.

Jeanine faced her. "I am certain of it. Linda and Dorothy are speaking badly about you. Fiona, too, I wager," she added in a dark tone.

"Why would they?" Anne said. "What can they possibly say that would alienate these gentlemen? And why say anything at all? There are plenty of gentlemen seeking ladies."

"Because the gentlemen fawned all over you that first night," Jeanine said. "You're more beautiful than any other lady here."

That, Anne knew, was untrue. There were some very beautiful girls here. Jeanine was one. But leave it to Jeanine to be loyal to a fault. Still, something was wrong, and Anne couldn't escape the feeling that the girls Jeanine had named did have something to do with it.

The lights began to dim. Her heart fell. The respectable ball had ended. Anne spotted half a dozen servants weaving throughout the ballroom and snuffing out candles. They would extinguish more than half the candles, leaving the massive room with many shadows.

"It's time to leave," Jeanine said.

Anxiety knotted her stomach. Once she left the party, she would have to wait another week for the opportunity to find a suitable match. There had to be some way to prepare for the next week. She couldn't sit passively in Lady Peddington's parlor and sew, sip tea, and talk about the final upcoming ball. Even if she met a gentleman tonight or next week, what guarantee was there she would make a match? She couldn't wait to the last minute and simply hope to find a husband. The candles on the table behind them were snuffed, leaving them standing in soft shadows.

Jeanine tugged on her arm. "Come along, Anne."

Dare she stay? Anne scanned the ballroom. At least one hundred and fifty guests, including Lady Paddington's girls, had attended the night's ball. Half of those had left. Anne counted ten graduates of Lady Paddington's School for Young ladies amongst the guests. Some had even removed their gloves. Three girls stood far too close to gentlemen, and the orchestra struck up a waltz. The Midnight Ball had officially begun.

Two gentlemen looked their way.

"Oh dear," Jeanine whispered. "Two gentlemen are headed our way. If we hurry, we can avoid them."

Anne faced Jeanine. "Quickly, you go on. I'll be up later."

"Nae, you need a husband with money," Jeanine's whisper grew urgent. "These men can offer you nothing."

Jeanine might not be correct. Some courtesans received very expensive gifts. Might she receive enough expensive gifts to support her estate for the next three years? Her mother had a good head for business. She could manage the tenants while Anne earned the money it would take to plant and harvest three years of crops. After that, Dover Hall could support itself *and* Castle Dòmnallach.

But that required substantial money…

The two gentlemen reached them and stopped closer than propriety allowed. But then, this was the Midnight Ball. Propriety had exited along with all the proper ladies.

The gentleman who stopped in front of Jeanine gave a slight bow. "May I have the honor of this dance?"

Jeanine glanced at Anne.

"Go on up to your room," Anne said. "I will be up later." She glimpsed the satisfied gleam in the eyes of the man standing near her.

"Just one dance, my dear," Jeanine's admirer urged.

Jeanine narrowed her eyes on Anne. "If you're staying, then I am staying." She looked at the gentleman. "I am happy to dance with you."

Before Anne could object, Jeanine slipped her hand into the

crook of the man's arm and allowed him to lead her toward the dance floor.

Anne hesitated. She should go after her. Oh, this was a terrible mess.

"Would you care for a walk in the garden, love?"

Anne looked sharply at the man standing uncomfortably close. She had no experience with men who were seeking mistresses, but she had been the object of male attention since the age of fourteen. Six years was long enough to gain some understanding of male passions. Only twice before had a gentleman referred to her with a personal endearment—outside of her father, of course. The first, was the boy she fell in love with at sixteen. They fell out of love a year later, but remained friends to this day. The other time mirrored tonight. The intimacy hadn't been earned, and evoked a sense of uneasiness that made her skin crawl.

Was this how a courtesan felt? Could she give the most private part of herself to a man who viewed her as nothing more than an object to serve his pleasure? Memories rose of her mother sitting before the hearth at Dover Hall, sewing on a cool autumn evening and her sister, Louisa, racing into the room with a drawing to show them or a passage from a favorite book she wanted to share, and the answer was a resounding yes.

But did that mean a walk in the garden?

Once they reached the cover of darkness, what would stop this man from taking what he wanted and then not paying for her charms? She flushed hot at her thoughts, but shoved aside the shame. How did a courtesan go about getting a man to offer a contract? The answer came more easily than she liked. She must tease just enough to entice him to offer a contract—a good contract.

Anne slanted her head and looked up at the man through her lashes. "Perhaps, sir, it would be better if we began with a dance. A walk in the gardens might be something for people who are on more...intimate terms."

A corner of his mouth lifted, and dread seeped through her. "My dear, I have no qualms about counting myself among the fortunate number of your lovers, but I have no intention of being the man who finances them."

Anne blinked. "I-I beg your pardon?" Her thoughts whirled. Finances *them*? She drew a sharp breath. "You think that I am looking for a protector and want to take lovers at his expense?"

He leaned closer and she stiffened when he traced a finger up her arm. "After we have enjoyed ourselves, I *might* introduce ye to a man who will look the other way when you take lovers while under his protection."

Her mind cleared. "You believe I will trade my-my—for a—" words failed as fury clouded her thinking. She arched a brow. "A walk in the garden, you say? You like the dark, sir?"

"Like it?" he said with a growl. "I prefer it."

Men were fools.

This time, she met his gaze squarely. "In my experience, a man who prefers the cover of darkness to make love to a woman is a man who is lacking in the proper—" she gave him a cool smile "—*tools* to please a lady."

He blinked, then his mouth thinned. "The gentlemen you draw into your web are most fortunate."

She lifted her chin. "You will not count yourself amongst their ranks."

It seemed he would say more, but he spun on his heel and strode away.

Anne released a deep breath, then realized a nearby group of men were staring. God help her, by tomorrow, word will have spread through Edinburgh that one of Lady Peddington's graduates was available for the taking.

"You can't fully blame him, you know," drawled a deep male voice behind her.

Anne whirled to face the speaker, a tall man leaning against the wall. Good heavens, he was handsome. The blue eyes that started at her were made all the more blue by his raven dark hair.

"I beg your pardon?" she said.

"There is no denying that Niall is uncouth," he said. "But you can't fault him for speaking the truth."

The temper that had got her into far too much trouble over the course of her life—including just a moment ago—reared its ugly head once again. "You know nothing of the situation."

"Unlike Niall, I respect a woman who knows what she wants and isn't afraid to pursue it," he said without rancor.

She frowned. "What the devil are you talking about?"

"A woman has just as much right to pursue her pleasure as does a man," he said.

Then she understood. "Where did you get the idea that I'm seeking lovers?" She should have known better than to stay for the Midnight Ball.

"Are ye saying it isn't true?" he asked, but before she could answer, he added. "It seems to be a well-known fact."

"Something can be a fact only if it's true," she said with exasperation.

He laughed. "You just rejected Niall's advances by telling him that you won't add him to your list of lovers."

She gave a frustrated shake of her head. "I was angry."

He laughed. "There is no need to be coy. I meant what I said, I respect a woman who isn't afraid to go after what she wants."

Anne exhaled a breath in an effort to control her temper. "But you insist that what I want is a string of lovers. What in heaven would I do with them?"

He pushed away from the wall. "Perhaps I can be of help in demonstrating the benefits of having at least one lover."

She rolled her eyes. "That would completely undermine my plans."

"What might those plans be?"

"I fail to see how that is any of your business," she said.

He shrugged. "If I'm to help, I must know your plans."

"Help?" Anne narrowed her eyes. "If you intend to help in the same fashion as that other gentleman, no thank you."

"I would never be so uncouth," he said.

A twinge of hope surfaced.

"Niall should never have asked you to trade your charms for the possibility of introducing you to a man who might be interested in becoming your protector."

"What should he have done?" she asked cautiously.

The man took two steps closer and grasped her hand. The warmth of his fingers caught her off guard. Eyes locked with hers, he lifted her hand and brushed his lips across her fingers, then released her.

"A lady should always know what to expect from a gentleman."

Anne agreed completely.

"A woman as beautiful as you should expect nothing less than a diamond bracelet after an intimate evening."

She stiffened. He didn't intend to make her his mistress. He intended to have her for one night, then send her home. *With a diamond bracelet*, her mind whispered. The situation had grown far more desperate than she could have imagined. Not only had she failed to capture the interest of a suitable prospect for a husband, she couldn't even interest a man in making her his mistress.

It made no sense. Men had vied for her attention—many, for her hand in marriage—since she'd turned sixteen. Now that she *needed* to marry, she was avoided. Quite a few men had approached her at Lady Peddington's first ball—or, at least the first half of the ball, now that she thought about it.

"Good heavens," she said under her breath. Jeanine was right. Someone had spread rumors about her. She regarded the gentleman. "Where did ye hear these things about me?"

"Men talk—just as women do, I wager."

"How dare they," she muttered.

"I beg your pardon?"

"They've ruined my chances of finding the right man."

"Perhaps I am the right man," he said.

She surveyed him, his raven hair, blue eyes, broad shoulders and long legs, then shook her head. "Nae, you are too handsome."

He blinked. "I had no idea being 'too handsome' was a drawback."

"It is for my purposes."

"I promise you, my dear, it isn't."

She gave a frustrated shake of her head. "A man like you has no need of a mistress, much less a wife."

His expression remained impassive. "Are those the only choices?"

She narrowed her eyes. "There you have it. I am correct. You are looking for a woman who will entertain you for an evening and then leave her with some silly trinket."

"I assure you, I never give 'silly trinkets' to ladies."

Nervous laughter emanated from somewhere in the shadows to Anne's right, but she kept her attention on the man. "How expensive is the jewelry that you would give?"

He lifted a brow. "Are we negotiating?"

Anne suddenly felt certain the conversation was going all wrong for a courtesan searching for a protector. Still, she said, "Call it curiosity."

Amusement appeared in his eyes. "Just the other day, I happened to see a particularly lovely gold bracelet and was saddened by the fact that I had no one to give it to. The bracelet would cost me two hundred pounds."

That meant she might sell it for one hundred pounds, if she were lucky. Her stomach knotted tighter. A man and woman glided past them.

Anne shook her head. "Such a small gift would do me no good."

His gaze sharpened. "What would do you some good?"

She waved him off. "I have no time to waste when you are offering me a bauble for my trouble."

"Trouble?" he repeated, then laughed again, this time full, rich and with amusement.

To her horror, warmth rippled through her. He stepped closer. So close, she caught a whiff of the sandlewood soap he'd used to bathe. But unlike Niall, he made no move to touch her, and her desire to step back wasn't out of revulsion, but a desire to hide the blush that warmed her cheeks. Good Lord, the man was charming.

"I promise ye, my lady, that you will not consider a night with me 'trouble.'"

The spell broke. Anne narrowed her eyes. "I see, I am to consider myself fortunate to have a night with you, and grateful for the bonus of a gold bracelet."

"I don't think that's quite what I said."

"It is exactly what you said," she retorted. "It's the height of arrogance for a man to think that a woman should thank him for bedding her."

His expression cooled. "I believe it is you who *asked* me to thank you with a gold bracelet."

She drew a sharp breath. He was right. Still… "Aye, but you act as if some of that payment should come in the form of gratitude for being fortunate enough to be chosen for your one night of-of…" she was at a loss for words.

"*Affaire d'amour?*" he drawled.

She snorted. "One night can hardly be called an affair and has nothing whatsoever to do with love."

"Is that what you want, my lady, love?"

"A woman always wants love. Well, love doesn't put food on the table." She read the surprise in his eyes and realized she'd lost control of the situation. "Take yourself off to some other woman who is willing to sell herself for a gold bracelet," she said. "I have a business to attend to."

KENNEDY DOUGLAS, VISCOUNT BUCHANAN, ENTERED HIS STUDY and the erotic fantasy of the ravishing beauty at Lady Peddington's ball lying on his sheets beneath him vanished at sight of his stepmother seated on the divan near the window. She sat straight—the proper wife—her honey-brown hair swept off her shoulders in a carefully coiffured mound atop her head. Her ivory evening dress, befitting a thirty-year-old woman, hugged her trim, perfect curves. Too bad her husband had one foot in the grave.

"What fresh hell has brought you here at this time of night, Jacqueline?"

"I realize it is after one in the morning," she said, "but I have been waiting since nine."

He had indulged a little too much in the free-flowing champagne at the ball, but the presence of his father's wife in his study at one forty-five in the morning dictated that he have something stronger than champagne to drink. He crossed to the sideboard where sat half a dozen decanters filled with various liquors, and poured himself a liberal dose of scotch. He put the top back on the decanter, picked up the glass, and turned.

He leaned against the sideboard. "Short of forcibly throwing you out, I suppose I can't stop you from telling me what the earl wants. Unless, that is, I simply retire to my bedchambers." Kennedy sipped his scotch and watched her over the edge of the glass. "Would you be bold enough to follow me, if I did?"

"I am here on an errand for your father, nothing more," she replied.

"Of course. You won't risk him questioning your faithlessness with his death so close at hand."

"Really, Kennedy. Must you always be so cruel?"

He gave her a cold smile. "With you, my sweet, I am afraid so. I know I'll regret asking, but what is so important that you waited nearly five hours to tell me? I know it isn't that my father is dead, for you would have hazarded the gates of hell to find me, if that were the case." He took another drink of whisky. The pleasant burn comforted. "Not to mention, you're not smiling."

"It really is unkind of you to continue to imply that I will be happy when your father dies."

"As I said, with you, there is no other way. What do you want?"

She reached into her reticule, withdrew a piece of paper, and looked up at him. "This is from your father."

He gave a mirthless laugh. "You could've left that on my desk. Better yet, you could have sent it by messenger. Why are you here?"

"Since you refuse to see your father, he sent me with this message, and instructed me to wait for a reply."

Kennedy finished the scotch and turned to refill the glass. "As I have no desire to see my father, what could induce me to read his letter?"

She sighed, then the rustling of a paper followed, and she said, "Kennedy, I imagine you will not deign to touch a paper that I have touched. No matter. If you force Jaqueline to read this, it will be all the worse for you. I am dying. But you know that."

Kennedy poured a double dose of liquor.

"I have commanded you to marry," Jacqueline went on, "but you go about your business as if you have no responsibility to me, the title, or our position in society. I believe that you have not married—will not marry—just to spite me. But I cannot allow your vendetta to bring an end to our line. I know threats of cutting you off from my money are meaningless. You would rather live in squalor than do a single thing I ask. Therefore, you leave me no choice."

Kennedy slowed in sliding the decanter top back on the decanter.

"You will marry within the week" --Kennedy released the decanter top as she finished the sentence— "or I will marry your sister to Lord Granbury ten days from now on her sixteenth birthday."

Kennedy whirled. "What the bloody hell?"

Jacqueline said, "There is more. 'You might think to make off with your sister and hide her somewhere, which is why I have already sent her away. No one save myself knows where she is. If I die tomorrow, no one will know where to look for her.'"

Kennedy stared. "This is insanity."

Jacqueline didn't shift her eyes from the letter, but continued, "I will not settle for a betrothal. You must marry and produce an heir within a year. Do so, and I will allow you to choose your sister's husband when the time comes. Defy me, and I will not only marry her and Granbury, but they shall not return home until she has produced an heir for him."

Kennedy dashed his glass against the hearth and took two steps toward Jacqueline. "This reeks of your handiwork."

She shook her head. "You underestimate your father, and overestimate my influence."

"I know you both too well to mistake either of you," he snarled.

"What possible reason could I have for wanting to see you

married?" She dropped her gaze. "I had always hoped…" She raised her head, eyes shimmering with moisture.

"By God," he exploded, "you missed your calling. You should have been an actress. Pray, do not pretend you have any tender feelings for me. Those illusions were shattered the day you rose from my bed and announced your engagement to my father." He snorted in derision. "I suppose I should thank him for marrying you. Though had he any idea that he was saving me from making the greatest mistake of my life, I'm sure he wouldn't have done it."

A tear slipped down her cheek.

Rage rammed through him. He crossed the room, seized her wrist and yanked her to her feet. "Where is Rose?"

She shrank back and shook her head. "I don't know. As the letter states, only he knows. He wouldn't chance my telling you." More tears slid down her cheeks. "He knows that you and I are close."

Kennedy released her and staggered back two paces. "Of course, he knows. That's why he married you."

She shook her head. "Nae, he does not know that we were —" she broke off

"Lovers?" he sneered.

"We were much more than that." She took a step toward him.

He turned away, his steps faltering, and reached his desk in time to brace himself, his back to her. "Leave, Jacqueline."

"Please, Kennedy, we cannot leave things like this between us."

"There is no *us*," he said.

Her skirts rustled and he realized she was walking toward him. He whirled to find her three steps away. He had to get away from her. Kennedy strode to the door. Hand on the knob, he looked back at her. "I suggest you not return home to your husband for at least an hour."

Half an hour later, Kennedy banged on the door of his father's townhome. The door opened in two seconds. Somewhere in the recesses of his mind, he realized the footman had been waiting for him. He pushed past the man and raced up the stairs to his father's bedchamber. The door stood open. Aye, his father expected him. He continued inside and found his father propped up in bed. A fission of alarm shot through him at sight of his father's yellow pallor. He looked far worse than when Kennedy had last seen him a year ago. Cruel fate. Only an hour ago, he would have rejoiced in seeing his father's decline. Now, until Rose was safely home, his father's illness frightened him more than anything ever had in his life.

The earl laid aside the book he'd been reading and met Kennedy's gaze.

"Where is she?" Kennedy demanded.

"Once you are married—to a proper lady, mind you, no peasant from the country—and once you produce an heir, I will bring her home," he replied in a strong voice that belied his appearance.

Kennedy's hands worked into fists at his sides. "I will kill you for this."

"Then you will never find your sister."

"She is not a child. She can find her way home." But she was a child. Only fifteen.

His father's gaze remained locked with his. "Do you really think I would make it that easy?"

Rage threatened to overwhelm him. His thoughts jumbled. His sister, only fifteen years old, being held prisoner somewhere. Would her jailers safeguard her?

Kennedy swayed. "How do I know she is safe?"

"She will always be safe under my care," his father replied.

"Your threat to marry her to Granbury proves otherwise," he snarled. "You know full well he beat his first wife to death."

"You are intelligent enough to know that gossip rarely resembles true events," the earl replied.

"I'm intelligent enough to know that most gossip has some grain of truth to it. If one hair on her head is harmed, I will kill you."

"You're threatening a dying man, Kennedy. I have made peace with my imminent death."

"You could live another year, to three or four. I can end you before that. I can end you tonight."

"Then you would never see your sister again."

"What happens if you die before I can produce an heir?" His heart thundered.

"I suggest you pray that doesn't happen."

Kennedy stared. His father was a bastard, but this went beyond anything Kennedy could have imagined the old man capable of. "You cannot keep her prisoner forever. She will escape. She will return home. Your threat is unreasonable." The last, he said more for himself than his father.

"Your sister isn't in Scotland. Escape is nigh to impossible. Even if she did manage by some miracle to escape, she would have to journey home. She has no friends, no money, no escort." The last words were said with an emphasis that told Kennedy his father knew the exact picture that had arisen in Kennedy's mind at the thought of his young sister trying to return home on her own. And she would try just that.

"You would sacrifice your daughter?" he whispered. "Risk her losing everything, possibly even her life, just to force me to marry?"

"You see my actions as those of a man bent on hurting you. I see my actions as those of a desperate man trying to preserve his legacy."

"Legacy?" Kennedy sneered. "I should have known. This has nothing to do with me. You don't give a damn if I marry or even carry on the title. This is about you wanting to be *remem-*

bered." Kennedy released a harsh breath. "If you wanted to extract revenge because I had Jacqueline before you did, I would have more respect for you. But this—" He shook his head. "You are right. These are the actions of a desperate man. You're a liar, Father. You do fear death." His father's eyes narrowed, but Kennedy gave him no chance to reply. "I will marry within a week. But only on one condition."

His father waited.

"Once you confirm my wife is with child, you will bring Rose home."

His father shook his head. "Your wife could lose the child, and the child might not be a male. I know you well enough to know that you wouldn't touch her again just to spite me."

Kennedy stared. "I would agree to the terms, if I were you. Keep in mind, I have considerable resources at my disposal. You know, of course, the moment I leave this house, I will begin my own search for Rose. If fortune favors me—and she often does—and I find my sister before you die, I will divorce my wife and immediately set about siring a string of bastards, none of whom can claim your title." Kennedy gave him a cold smile. "Then I will seduce your wife and sire a child on her that cannot possibly inherit your title."

His father's eyes widened. "You're not capable of such dastardly actions."

Kennedy gave him a cold smile. "I am capable of far worse. After all, I am your son."